# Praise for
# Maybe in Paris

"Set against the magic and possibility of Paris, Christiansen's emotional debut not only reminds us of the challenges that come with loving someone as they are, but also, the incomparable beauty."

—Ashley Herring Blake, author of *How to Make a Wish*

"A touching, relevant story about siblings, autism, and unconditional love. Beautifully written, compelling, and honest."

—Marci Lyn Curtis, author of *The One Thing*

"Readers will swoon over the delicious descriptions of Paris . . . but will ultimately find that Keira's emotional journey covers even more ground than her physical one, in a story that focuses on a complex, yet tender, sibling relationship."

—Jen Malone, author of *Wanderlost*

"*Maybe in Paris* captures all the excitement of youthful obsession—with a city or a boy—while offering a touching depiction of the bonds we too often take for granted. Few books about teen sibling relationships capture their ups and painful downs so frankly."

—Margot Harrison, author of *The Killer in Me*

"Heartbreaking but hopeful, *Maybe in Paris* is a wonderful debut with a beautiful setting, complicated, yet realistic sibling relationship, and a dash of romance."

—Chantele Sedgwick, author of *Love, Lucas* and *Switching Gears*

"Good YA depends on great voice, and Rebecca Christiansen brings it to bear. She announces herself as a voice to be reckoned with in the very first pages of *Maybe in Paris* and doesn't relent. A welcome debut sure to launch a million fans."

—Tom Leveen, author of *Shackled* and *Random*

# MAYBE IN PARIS

## REBECCA CHRISTIANSEN

Sky Pony Press
New York

Sky Pony Press books may be purchased in bulk at special discounts for sales promotion, corporate gifts, fund-raising, or educational purposes. Special editions can also be created to specifications. For details, contact the Special Sales Department, Sky Pony Press, 307 West 36th Street, 11th Floor, New York, NY 10018 or info@skyhorsepublishing.com.

Sky Pony® is a registered trademark of Skyhorse Publishing, Inc.®, a Delaware corporation.
Visit our website at www.skyponypress.com.

10 9 8 7 6 5 4 3 2 1

Library of Congress Cataloging-in-Publication Data is available on file.

Cover design by Sammy Yuen
Interior design by Joshua Barnaby

Print ISBN: 978-1-5107-0880-8
Ebook ISBN: 978-1-5107-0882-2

Printed in the United States of America

*To my brother, Scott, and my sister, Grace.
You guys are the reason Keira and Levi's relationship
is so full of both frustration and love.*

# MAYBE IN PARIS

# CHAPTER ONE

Footsteps thunder through my house in the early morning. My eyes snap open, weighted with eye shadow still caked on from prom.

"Levi!" my stepdad, Josh, shouts. "Oh God, Levi, oh God, no . . ."

He runs past my room and stumbles down the basement stairs, shouting my brother's name over and over and over.

Somehow, I already know what's happened.

Levi. Little brother. Dead.

Josh screams up the stairs for my mom. "Amanda! Amanda, call 911!"

I'm stiller than a statue. Somewhere in the house, Mom sobs.

Levi, the little brother I made snap yesterday. Whose sour mood ruined my prom photo shoot. Whose scraggly neck beard and 350-pound frame made Jacques St-Pierre, my date, snigger. Levi, the blemish. Oh God.

I fling off my blankets and tiptoe to my door.

"It's my son," Mom cries in the kitchen. "There was a note outside our bedroom door, and—and my husband is with him now . . ."

Mom's footsteps hurry down the basement stairs to Levi's bedroom. I strain my ears.

"Y-yes, yes, he's breathing. . . . I—I don't know, there was a note outside our bedroom door, there was a note . . ."

A note.

I stay just inside my bedroom door. Frozen. The quiet suburban cul-de-sac outside my window gradually fills with sirens. Flashing lights steep my room in red and blue. Strange voices invade my house. Paramedics maneuver equipment down the basement stairs, knocking against the walls. And still I stand here, too terrified to move.

One siren fades, bleeding into the early morning. Is that Levi, being taken away? I want to peek out my window, but my body won't let me. I contemplate hiding in my closet, burying my face in the yellow silk of my Marie Antoinette–inspired prom dress. Prom was a mess—I can't stop picturing Jacques's sheepish smirk and Selena's grin when I stumbled across them in the girls' bathroom, her lipstick all over his face—but compared to now, to *this*, it was a dream.

I could be losing my brother right now.

*Oh, God.*

The house is silent. The sun somehow rose.

I grab my robe, sneak down the hall—*don't look downstairs*—and into the big, open kitchen-slash-living room. It's full of morning light. Everything is normal. Except the silence.

Josh sits at the computer desk in the living room. His and Mom's computers face opposite directions, so they can stare lovingly into each other's eyes while their elf avatars battle orcs on *Stones of Zendar*, the online role-playing game where they met six years ago. Mom's embroidered portrait of their avatars, holding hands, presides on the wall above their computers.

Josh's face looks gray and drawn in the monitor light, and much older than his thirty-two years.

"Josh?" I whisper. "Is Levi okay?"

He looks up at me from the *Stones of Zendar* log-in page, which he's been staring at this whole time.

"You heard what happened?"

*I heard enough.* I nod. My body shakes, like it's containing a potential scream. I pray to God Josh doesn't tell me any specifics. If I hear about wounds, notes, or stomachs being pumped, my scream will break loose.

"Levi's in the hospital," Josh says, barely keeping control of his voice. "Your mom is with him. He's very, very sick, okay?"

"Okay," I whisper.

"We just need to wait." Josh lets out a shaky breath and returns to the log-in screen. He covers his face with his hands. I sit down on the couch and watch my sweaty fingers shake. I turn on the TV and put on this Louis XVI documentary I DVRed, but even at full blast, the jaunty harpsichord music doesn't drown out the sobs Josh tries and fails to smother.

# CHAPTER TWO

When I was getting ready for prom, the world still seemed bright, shiny, and full of possibilities. I was riding a new wave of the thrill I had gotten back in October when I'd first asked Jacques St-Pierre, devilishly handsome French exchange student, to be my prom date. Miraculously, as the year went on, Jacques hadn't broken it off and asked someone else instead. It had seemed like a dream all year, but it was *really happening*.

Maybe, I thought, if I could *finally* capture his heart tonight, I could tag along with him back to France. Over the past year, I'd saved up six thousand dollars from my cashiering job at Safeway, and I was determined to go with or without him—but "with" was preferable. "With" meant a free place to stay in France, at the very least. "With" meant a decent start to my plan for life post-high school and pre-college—my hopefully long career as a nomad in Europe, a professional wanderer. If Jacques joined me for that . . . yeah, that'd just be amazing.

It took three hours of makeup, hair styling, and dress fastening, but a French queen was finally staring me back in the mirror. I hadn't gone *full* Marie Antoinette. It was senior prom, not a historical reenactment. I would have preferred that, though; I could've gone for a sky-high powdered wig instead of my plain brown ringlets, which were the same as always, only all crunchy from hair spray.

Once I was ready, there was nothing to do but wait for Jacques to pick me up in the limo we were sharing with his friends. I sat on my bed and imagined the reaction that would blossom on his face when he saw how perfect I looked. The door would open, his eyes would fall on me, and his jaw would hit the floor. It would be like every other chick flick after the heroine gets a makeover and the hero sees how beautiful she truly is. As Marie Antoinette, the girl synonymous with his hometown—Versailles, France—I would be irresistible to him. He would look at me and feel like he was home. His eyes would never slide past me again.

"Keira!" my stepdad, Josh, had shouted up the stairs. "I think Jacques is here!"

A shock jolted up my spine and I jumped off my bed. I carefully stepped through my room, my skirt bumping and jostling every piece of furniture. I had to reach down and press the hoop in to fit through the doorway. I felt a twinge of impatience and annoyance, but I wore it like a badge of honor. This was the true Marie Antoinette experience.

I was at the top of the stairs when Josh opened the front door to reveal Jacques in his couture tux. He looked up in time to see me and my sumptuous skirt float down the stairs like a silken dream. I literally could not have planned the moment any better.

His eyes popped open; the color drained from his face.

"*Bon soir, Jacques*," I said in the best accent I could muster. "*Tu aimes ma robe?*" *You like my dress?*

His mouth opened, but he didn't answer. His sculpted eyebrows were raised to the max. After another second of failing to speak, a laugh escaped. He tried to stifle it but it squeaked out.

"Oh, shit," he said.

It wasn't "oh, shit" in a "you look amazing" kind of way. It was the kind of "oh, shit" you say when you drop a glass and it shatters. The kind of "oh, shit" that means "I screwed up." The kind that means "what have I gotten myself into?" Just remembering it, even two whole months later, mortification forms a pit in my stomach.

Josh noticed everything: Jacques's laugh, my frozen face. He jumped in to toss me a life preserver, but I was beyond saving.

"Well, hey there, Jacques! Don't you look dapper! Um, would you like a drink before you guys head off?"

"Eh . . ." Jacques said. He was trying to stop laughing, but he was failing. "Eh, no thank you. Um . . . *mon Dieu* . . ."

*My God.*

His eyes were fixed on my dress. My dress, which before had felt like perfection, like a dream come to life, felt like exactly what it was: too much. A cake I was popping out of like a cheap stripper. A try-hard effort to impress. Embarrassment incarnate.

"Aren't you a pair!" Mom's voice said from somewhere behind me. "Why don't you step inside, Jacques? I just want to take a few quick pictures."

"Uh, my friends, they are waiting," Jacques said, pointing to the limo parked on the street. The limo full of popular kids, the lion's den I dreaded stepping into.

"We'll be quick," Mom said, waving him inside. "Why don't you guys stand in front of the fireplace, there? Oh, should we put on the corsage and boutonnière first?"

Josh brandished the plastic case containing Jacques's boutonnière. I had spent an hour picking it out at the florist's the day before.

An hour that I realized was completely wasted when I saw Jacques hold up empty hands.

"I do not have a corsage," he said. "Sorry."

He wasn't sorry. He was still trying to suppress laughter. At least our red faces matched.

"They must not have that tradition in France," Josh said, a little too loud. "That's okay! Um, I'm sure we could make up a quick corsage for Keira from the garden."

You know a prom night is broken beyond repair when the savior of the night is your stepdad, not your date.

"Forget it," I blurted out. "Let's just take some pictures and get out of here."

Mom and Josh looked at each other. As Josh dragged the chairs away from the fireplace and Mom adjusted the camera, they chattered pointlessly, trying to ease the mood. I was grateful, but I wanted to just get the hell out. At least at prom, I could pretend all this had never happened. Here, I was trapped in this nightmare.

"Okay, get in there, lovebirds," she said. I winced. "Smile!"

I grinned, but the second the flash went off, I dropped the act. I was so done. I couldn't tell Jacques to get out and not go to prom—I had to save face in front of the assholes in the limousine—but I couldn't play along with the whole farce. He was *laughing* at me. The fragile wall of denial I'd built was crumbling. He had always been laughing at me, and I'd always known it, and facing that fact felt like swinging a hammer at my heart.

"What's the matter, Keira?" Mom asked.

"Let's just go," I said.

I headed for the door, but a few sudden sounds split the air. *Thumpthumpthump creeeeak.* My brother had stomped up the basement stairs and opened the door. I turned my head and saw him peek out, then emerge from the dark basement into the hall.

Levi looked huge—my brain bucked, not computing what it saw. It wasn't like I hadn't physically seen him in a long time; we lived in the same house, worked around each other in the kitchen all the time. His hulking form lurching down the hall, though, made me wonder when the hell he had grown up.

He dragged his enormous feet down the hallway, duck-footed toes scraping the carpet. He wore shorts that exposed his impossibly furry calves. Scraggly hair grew along his jawline and down his neck. His shoulders curled inward when he peered into the living room and saw Jacques.

*Fuck,* I thought. I didn't want Jacques to see him. My ghostly, basement-dwelling brother was yet another thing Jacques would find hilarious.

"Oh, hi, Levi!" Mom said.

Levi grunted and headed for the kitchen, shuffling as quickly as he could.

"Hey, Levi, I have an idea," Mom said. "Why don't we take a quick picture of you and Keira on her special day, since I have the camera out?"

Jacques turned to face the wall, his shoulders shaking. I clenched my fist.

I didn't know who I wanted to punch more: Jacques, who was an asshole, or Mom, who had latched onto this terrible idea. She was dragging Levi out of the kitchen by his arm. He was so hunched that if I didn't already know he was six-foot-three, I would think he was tiny.

"I don't have any pictures of the two of you together," she was saying.

"I don't want to," Levi grumbled.

"Amanda, don't force him," Josh said.

"It'll be quick." She steered Levi over to where I was standing. "Just stand next to your sister."

She pushed Levi in close—as close as my three-foot-radius skirt would allow. It bumped up against Levi's leg and he recoiled.

"Get in close, you two," Mom directed, raising the camera.

Levi hovered just out of range of my skirt, too far away for the picture. "I don't want your dress to touch me."

I waved Levi over impatiently. He shook his head. I took a step closer to him. My skirt brushed his legs again, and he staggered backward like it electrocuted him.

"Stop fucking touching me!" He brushed furiously at his legs, as if my skirt had left some powdery residue. "If you make it touch me again, I'll fucking burn it."

I snapped. "It's silk. How can you hate silk?"

"It's itchy." He was scratching his calves like I'd touched him with stinging nettle instead of silk ruffles.

"It's silk, it's not itchy."

"*I'll fucking burn it.*"

"Levi!" Mom gasped.

I became acutely aware of everything going on in the room at that moment. Mom had her camera raised, even as she gaped at Levi. Levi was glaring at the floor. Josh was standing awkwardly to the side, hands stretched out like he was getting ready to break up this cage match.

And Jacques was still over by the fireplace. He was pinching the bridge of his nose, like he was just trying to hold it together. Like it was all so fucking hilarious.

"Suck it up for two seconds, Levi, then I can get out of here," I snapped. I stepped resolutely closer to him and plastered on the biggest, fakest smile I could muster. In the picture, it would look like nothing was wrong. If we all succeeded in blocking this night from our memories, Future Us would look at this photo of Levi and I and think, "Aww, what a happy moment."

Unfortunately, Levi had other plans.

He roared, "*Get off me!*"

His arms thrust outward in a last, desperate attempt to get me away from him. His huge hands collided with my shoulder. Unsteady on my high heels, I toppled over.

My dress cushioned most of my fall—except for my head, which smacked the stone ledge of the fireplace.

Pain exploded outward from the impact. The edges of my vision went black, manic exploding stars filled the in-between, but I managed to hold on to consciousness.

"Oh my God, Keira." Josh pushed a chair over, making his way toward me. "Are you okay? Keira, talk to me."

I managed to slur out that I was okay. Mom was screaming at Levi.

9

"What was that?! Why would you do that, Levi? Come back here! You think you can just walk away after that? *Come back here and apologize to your sister!*"

Levi had disappeared back downstairs. Jacques? He just stood there, dumbfounded, the remains of a smirk still on his face.

I don't know why I insisted on getting up, shaking it off, and going to prom. I had every excuse to stay home: an aching head, the stars that still lingered in my vision, vague nausea. But no, I picked myself up, grabbed Jacques, and went out to the limo. I endured the chattering of the two other couples in there with us—Selena Henderson and Mark Wasserman, and Callie White and Justin Landau—while biting my lip and trying not to cry. I toughed it out through the mortification of my eighteenth-century monstrosity standing out from everyone else's sleek, sexy sheath dresses. The chaperones and moms were the only ones who complimented it; everyone else just raised an eyebrow.

And I suffered through losing sight of Jacques after just a few minutes of the actual party, then walking into the girls' bathroom to find him making a hickey on Selena Henderson's neck with her perched on the counter, pressed against the mirror. I got their bashful, but unashamed looks as a reward for making it through the horrible night so far.

"It's not like you guys were dating," Selena said, panting hard. "You're not even his type, Keira."

Jacques nodded and admitted, "*Trop grosse.*"

*Too big.*

I took one look at him, with his hands clutching her skinny thighs, and walked out. Out the door, through the parking lot. I would have walked home, along the freeway if I'd had to, but one of the chaperones caught me by the arm and called Mom to come pick me up.

Jacques is dead to me now. When I think about him—aside from the huge cloud of pain I tamp back down inside me—all I can think about are the months I wasted pursuing him. I could've been doing literally anything else, but I chose to pour countless hours into this douchebag, who only liked me as a chauffeur and lip service provider.

When I went to bed that night, head sore and smeared makeup still all over my face, I thought the worst had already happened.

I had no idea.

# Chapter Three

If you had asked me on prom night what I thought I'd be doing two months from then, I would have answered with two words: "Paris" and "Jacques."

My original summer plan had been to go to France with Jacques when he went home, and after a good couple weeks in Paris, the city of my soul, traipse through the streets of every European metropolis. But summer is coming to a close, and the whole time, I've been stuck in Shoreline, Washington, which is also known as Hell. Jacques wasn't going to make or break the plan; I would still have gone without him. The loss of some jerk couldn't destroy my ideal summer.

The near loss of my brother, though . . . that could.

We're all drowning in the aftermath of what happened the night of my prom. Josh has become a silent warrior, going to work and taking care of the chores and errands that keep us afloat. I go to work at Safeway, come home, and head straight for my room. I ignore my friends' texts and invitations to hang out, letting those relationships fade like they were bound to the minute we graduated high school. I dodge Mom's attempts at lectures and conversations, cover my ears as she shouts information about Levi up the stairs. I sit up there all night, every night, wrapping myself in denial and watching Netflix until I pass out. Repeat it all the next day. It's all a blur.

All I really remember in detail is that I tried to write a poem the day after Levi was taken away. That used to help when I was being ignored by a crush, or turned down when I finally confessed my feelings to him. I pressed the pen against the page of my journal, but I couldn't make it move. All I ended up with was one dot poking a hole through the page. I couldn't make sense of my pain enough to describe it.

Mom has taken time off from her legal assistant career to become a walking, talking bundle of nerves. She spends every day she's allowed at Levi's treatment center, including the day of my graduation. Josh and an empty chair witnessed me cross the stage in my cap and gown. Every day, Mom asks if I'll go with her to see Levi, and every day, I have an excuse.

At first, I wasn't allowed to visit. The doctors said too many visitors in the first week could be overwhelming for Levi, and they wanted to minimize his stress. It was easy to say "okay, I won't go" when it was what they wanted, but now that I'm allowed and even encouraged to go, I feel paralyzed. I am terrified to visit Levi, so scared of what I might see. The truth is, I'm still adjusting to a world where my brother almost stopped existing. In some alternate universe, some version of me has to face the rest of her life as an only child, drowning in guilt because she didn't stop this, didn't see it coming. Just imagining that world makes my palms sweat. This world, where Levi survived, feels fragile and liable to collapse. If I go and see Levi, what if it makes him worse? What if he tries to . . . leave again?

But last night, after another screaming, tearful reprimand from my mom, I finally gave in. Today, I'm going to the treatment center where Levi has been since the morning after my prom. Since he wrote a good-bye note and swallowed three-quarters of a bottle of aspirin. My sixteen-year-old brother was mentally packed and ready to go, ready to blow a hole in our lives, ready to stop existing. Ready and *wanting* to . . .

If I even think about it, my eyes fill with tears. I can't cry in front of Mom, as a matter of principle. I think about the price of a ticket out of here instead. This morning: Seattle to Paris, one adult, one way, $564.

"Levi might be grouchy this morning," Mom says as we exit the freeway. Since we left home, she's talked nonstop about Levi's medical situation—the information I've been tuning out all summer. She's really letting me have it now that she's got me cornered. "He's adjusting to a new medication. If you see him making any weird facial expressions, let the doctors know right away. This medication could cause him to develop muscle tics that could become permanent."

I wish I'd tuned this out, too. What the hell am I going to see, walking into that hospital room? Fear ties my stomach in knots.

"Just talk to him," she says. "Ask him how the hospital has been. See if you can get him to talk about the book he's reading. He doesn't like to talk about that stuff with me. But with you, maybe."

She talks about the tests they've done on him and the diagnoses they're throwing around—"autism with signs of developing schizophrenia or bipolar disorder." Those words, they're so harsh. You picture Hollywood mental hospitals, patients drooling in straightjackets. My little brother can't be that far gone, just can't be. He took a downward spiral, I know that—dropping his friends, skipping school, then transferring to alternative school, then online school, then refusing to ever leave our basement—but my brain refuses to accept that he's as broken as she says. If he is, when did he break, and where was I?

I know that answer. Whenever Levi started to spiral, I was out the door and headed in chase of whatever boy I was besotted with that week. Hiding from Levi the Problem, deluding myself into thinking it was okay, he didn't need me.

Well, he wasn't okay, and he did need me. Guilt has broken through my mental barrier and is seeping into my bones. It's like I just woke up and saw the world for the first time. I don't like what I see. I don't like who I've become.

But I'm not ready for Mom to rub my face in it.

"I'm glad you're finally coming," she says as we're stuck in freeway traffic. The word *finally* drips with emphasis.

I swallow hard and watch the lines on the road creep slowly past. Wish I could escape the car as easily as they slip away.

"You've been absent the past few months, Keira," Mom says. "Your brother's life has gone to shit, and you were off gallivanting with your boyfriend. Who, I'm sorry, didn't even turn out to be worth your time."

My eyes well up with tears. "Mom, he—"

"There's no excuse, Keira. I've wanted to tell you all this for quite some time, so don't interrupt me now." She takes a deep breath and plunges deeper. "Romantic relationships, at your age, mean nothing. Family is everything. I know boys say nice things, and it feels like you're the first girl to ever hear those things, but believe me, you're not."

I blink and the tears spill over. Mom continues listing all the other ways I'm disappointing—choosing language and art classes over physics and calculus, deferring college, my messy bedroom, unfolded laundry. It all comes out, a tornado of hurtful words.

"You were always such a nice girl, Keira," she says with a sigh. "Even though you made some bad choices. I could forgive irresponsibility if you just kept being a good girl. You don't know how disappointing it is to learn that your daughter would drop everything just because some boy complimented her. It's a bit . . . slutty. I'm sorry, but it's true."

I'm full-on sobbing now. I feel like I've crashed against rock bottom. It would be one kind of pain if she was right. If my mother was calling it like it is on a set of facts, I could deal with that. Her being wrong, not even caring to find out the truth, makes it hurt even worse. Makes me want to hurt her back.

"Mom, I'm a *virgin*," I said through my tears. "I've never even been *kissed*. Jacques straight-up told me I'm too fat to be his type. But even if I had slept with him, or a million guys, I can't believe you would throw that in my face."

She sits in silence, hopefully reeling from the shock, but I can't make myself look at her to check. The windshield wipers flick back and forth, the engine rattles. We creep forward in the traffic. The thought of jumping out and walking home on the glass-strewn shoulder of the freeway is weirdly appealing.

"Oh," Mom says.

I hold my breath, waiting for more, but nothing else comes. She's not even going to apologize? Then again, I don't think she's ever apologized to me, so I don't know why I'm surprised.

"I didn't say that to be mean." Her voice comes out rushed—she's thinking as she's speaking. Never a good sign. "I just mean that you're smart, Keira. You can really make something of your life. I'm scared you're going to fall head over heels for some idiot, get pregnant, and end up struggling your whole life."

"Like you did?"

I almost slap my hand over my mouth. I honestly didn't mean to say it; it just popped out. Mom stomps on the brakes, but it's her only reaction to my horrible, cruel words. I have a right to be angry—my mom straight-up called me a slut! And implied that I'd pick the wrong guy and ruin my life forever, because she apparently thinks I'm stupid, too—but I already regret saying that.

"Actually, yes," she says. "Like I did."

She probably thinks that's the ultimate olive branch. *Oh, Mommy, you compared me to your young-and-dumb self and implied that*

*I have to be your vicarious wish fulfilment and live my life according to what you always wanted for yourself! All is truly mended between us!*

"Keira, I had big, big plans, but I threw them away because a boy said all the right things. I won't let you do that, too. You're already dangerously close, what with deferring college for this half-baked Europe idea."

I sigh. "It always comes back to college with you, doesn't it? I've told you this a million times. I will go, eventually."

The traffic light ahead of us turns red. She stomps on the brakes again, a little too late—the nose of the car pokes into the intersection. "You don't know how big of a mistake you're making. Why can't you wait to travel? Can't you buckle down, get undergrad under your belt before you run off and play? You need work ethic to survive in the real world, Keira, and you're not going to get that by screwing around in foreign countries."

*Screwing around.* My vision flashes red as we pull back into traffic. For a second, I imagine waiting to go to France until I had finished four whole years of college. I feel pain, literal pain, deep in my chest, and a wave of nausea. I can't do it. I can't wait four whole years to see Paris. It would be as impossible as waiting four years to eat. If I were to wait, the opportunity would slip through my fingers, maybe even disappear entirely. How often have you heard people say "I'm glad I waited until I was settled to travel!"? Never. I need to go, and I need to go as soon as humanly possible.

And she calls that *screwing around.* My soul is screaming for something—I don't know what, but I know Paris is the key—and Mom calls the idea of answering its call "screwing around." To her, art, architecture, history, the pursuit of knowledge and the quest after beauty are trivial. Unimportant. Something you put off until your taxes are done and your suburban lawn is neatly trimmed. To her, plunging into life and adventure and my own heart is nonessential nonsense. She doesn't understand the beauty of being lost, and the wonder of being found. I don't either yet, but the difference is that I want to.

And somehow, this woman raised me. I somehow rose up out of all her bad choices and banality and slut-shaming shallowness. Well, I'll rise above all that. Like a phoenix or some shit.

I bet nothing hurts phoenixes. I still have tears in the corners of my eyes.

The traffic speeds up and we finally take our exit off the freeway. Mom's silence continues. We turn off at a sign that reads MORNINGSIDE YOUTH TREATMENT CENTER and park in a big lot. Once she kills the engine, Mom finally tries to say, "Keira, I'm—"

"Save it," I interrupt. "If you're not really sorry, don't apologize."

My heart really breaks when she doesn't try again.

The treatment center is beautiful; even in my battered emotional state, I can appreciate it. Floor-to-ceiling windows let in light, nurses smile, colorful murals fill the walls. Mom says hi to a receptionist and walks in, knowing exactly where she's going.

Levi's room is at the end of a hall.

A few doorways away, I balk. Mom walks into the room like it's no big deal. She knows what she's going to see.

When I think of Levi, I think of rubber boots, his footwear of choice since he was a toddler. Toy Godzillas, plural, because one wasn't enough. Sweaty Xbox controllers, from when he and I would stay up all night playing games we knew were too stupid and juvenile for us. It wasn't even that long ago—we were still playing Shrek and Lego Harry Potter games when I was fifteen and getting caught up in Henri, my first French exchange student obsession. Levi and I became separate entities instead of one-and-the-same. I abandoned him.

What am I going to see, walking into his room now? My brother, or a ghost of him, haunted by medication and those words: *mentally ill, autistic, schizophrenic.*

I finally take a deep breath, turn the corner, and walk in. I see Josh, focused on the TV in the corner. He's sitting next to the bed. And then I find Levi.

Levi slumps against his pillows. He's wearing a zombie T-shirt (normal) and gray sweatpants (also normal). His auburn hair is messy and tangled (normal), but it looks clean (very abnormal). His glasses are their usual combination of crooked and dirty. He looks bigger than I remember, in every way: taller, wider, and much, much heavier. When did he get so tall that his clown feet dangle off the end of the bed? When did his shoulders reach linebacker width? When did his hands become huge mitts, and when did the stomach they perch on get so large? Where did the "little" part of "little brother" go, and how could I not have noticed it fading away?

"I hate *Deadliest Warrior*," Levi says in a deep monotone. "Why the hell would Napoleon and George Washington ever fight each other one-on-one? They're generals, not fucking foot soldiers. Give them each a couple thousand men and a proper battlefield and then you could maybe call one of them the winner."

Mom laughs once, but it's strained. She says, "Levi, your sister is here."

Levi looks up at me. He grunts once.

"Hi, Lev," I say. "How's it going?"

"Good, I guess."

Nothing else. I just nod. Mom and Josh look at each other.

"Why don't Josh and I go get something to eat?" Mom says. "You guys can make fun of this silly show together."

I sit in the chair Josh left empty. The *Deadliest Warrior* episode trucks on toward its stupid finale, and Levi watches it in silence. His hands are clenched in fists on his lap. I can't stop staring at him. I should be talking to Levi, trying to cheer him up or whatever. Nothing more meaningful comes to mind than "How's it going?"

"I told you," he answers. "Good."

"What have you been up to?"

"Hospital stuff?" he says, like *duh?* But the irritation fades when he says, "I had an MRI the other day."

An MRI? Isn't that what they do for people with brain tumors? I try to respond as though I'm not totally freaking out. "Oh, yeah? What was that like?"

"Loud. Annoying. 'Cause you have to be completely still."

"Yeah?"

"Yeah."

I chew the inside of my cheek. "Um, did they find anything?"

"Dunno yet. But that room, where they had the MRI machine? It had these cool ceiling tiles."

"Yeah?"

"Yeah. Probably the most interesting ceiling I've seen here so far."

I smile, feeling like I've stepped back in time. *This* is the old Levi. This is the kid whose bedroom I would sneak into in the middle of the night to secretly watch *Austin Powers* or *Teenage Mutant Ninja Turtles*. The poking and prodding under microscopes and MRI machines hasn't erased him. He didn't go anywhere.

Now it really hits me that, two months ago, I almost lost him.

"Oh, *Mythbusters* is on next." Levi grabs the remote and turns up the volume. "Why do they even have shows like this on the History Channel, anyway?"

I laugh, but my voice is full of almost-tears. I hope he can't hear that. Crying pisses him off.

We watch the opening minutes of *Mythbusters* in silence, and during the first commercial break, Levi says, "So when are you leaving?"

"I thought I'd just stay until Mom wanted to go. Or if you want me to leave earlier, I could probably go home with Josh."

"No, like, to Europe."

"Oh! Um. I don't have any plans yet."

His lips twist around and pucker into his mouth. He does that when he's either about to lie, tell a joke, or deciding whether to say something. What's it going to be?

"I thought you were leaving soon," he says.

"I don't think so. Not when you're . . ."

*In recovery for trying to kill yourself.* I swallow the words.

"When you go, you should visit Chernobyl," Levi says. "It's almost safe there now. You just need a Geiger counter and a guide who knows the terrain."

I smile. "That sounds cool."

He grunts. In approval, I guess.

"I saw this thing about how the trees there are bringing radiation out of the ground when they grow up. And their fruit is poisoned and stuff."

"Scary."

"Yeah."

We watch some more *Mythbusters* until Mom and Josh come back in with coffee.

"How's it going, guys?" Mom asks. Her eyes go big and round and doe-like as she pulls up a chair facing me and Levi.

Josh sits facing the TV. "They're trying to walk on water?" he says, chuckling.

"Yeah." Levi forces the word out like it hurts him, his scowl returning.

"Dr. Pearson should be stopping in soon, Levi," Mom says. "Do you want Keira to be here for that? We could have a big family meeting."

He doesn't say anything.

Eventually a nurse comes and we all follow her to a "counselling room." It looks onto the garden in the courtyard, and we wait about half an hour before Dr. Pearson finally arrives.

"Hello, hello," he says as he strides in. He shakes Mom's hand, then Josh's, then mine. "You must be the sister?"

I say yes and "nice to meet you," then Dr. Pearson sits down. He hasn't so much as glanced at Levi, who sits next to him at our round table, hands folded over his big belly.

"So we're on Praxicet and Trioxate," Dr. Pearson says, reading off the papers in front of him, "to balance mood and get those depression symptoms under control. Other levels are consistently good, Levi's in decent physical health, apart from needing to drink more water and eat more veggies, but we're working on that. How have you found him lately?"

He directs the question at Mom. She leans forward as she answers, like she's speaking into a microphone.

"Fine," she says. "Sleepy, though."

"That's a typical side effect," Dr. Pearson drawls, leaning back in his chair. "But I think we're on a roll at the moment. Behavior is normal. The antipsychotic, Risperdal, seems be having a great effect, but I might want to switch him to Promidal just to see . . ."

*Antipsychotic?* Switching drugs "just to see"? As though Levi's just a lab experiment, a little white mouse he can do horrible, unnatural things to, "just to see"? Dr. Pearson goes on and on, detailing all his plans to turn my brother into a cocktail of medications. He sounds like a little kid talking about his chemistry set, not a doctor with real control over someone's life—someone who is sitting right there, big brown eyes cast downward, saying nothing, betraying no emotion. I want to open the cage and scoop that little lab mouse out, cradle him to my chest, protect him.

My relief at seeing the old Levi disappears, because what if it's temporary? What if all these drugs drain him away?

"Well, if nobody has any other questions or concerns . . ." Dr. Pearson stands up to leave.

"Um, Doctor," Mom says. "I actually had a question."

He sits back down, sighing, as if this could take all day. I hate him.

"Um . . . I've wanted to ask . . . how does the future look for Levi? He's only sixteen, but when he turns eighteen, nineteen . . . how do you think he'll be able to cope in the real world?"

Levi blinks slowly. There might not be any emotion in his eyes, but there's curiosity. He's listening.

You'd better have something good to say, Dr. Douchebag.

"Honestly, Mrs. Braidwood, most of the patients I've seen at Levi's age don't grow into what you and I would consider functioning young adults. Take your daughter, here." He gestured at me. "What, eighteen years old? Off to college, moving into the sorority house?"

I fight the urge to gag at the thought of joining a sorority. Dr. Pearson is nowhere near as omniscient as he thinks himself.

He continues. "From what I've seen of Levi here, depending on his ability to cope with his illness moving forward, he may need to remain in your custody as an adult. College may be out of the question, and depending on whether or not he can develop more effective communication skills, he may not ever be capable of living alone."

Levi's face still shows no emotion. That's okay—I'm full of enough anger for the two of us.

Mom nods. "Thank you, Dr. Pearson."

"You're welcome," he says with a debonair smile. He's already leaving the room. "Nice to meet you, big sister. Go, Tigers!"

*What?* I glance at Josh. He looks just as baffled as I am.

⚬⚬⚬

"Maybe he meant Tony the Tiger," Josh considers as we sit in freeway traffic on the drive home. "Maybe you just look like someone who loves Frosted Flakes."

Laughing feels good after this stupid day, even if it's at a painfully unfunny dad joke. I put my feet in their flip-flops up on the dashboard in front of me. Mom would never allow me to fold my body up right in front of the airbag like this. *What if we crashed?!* Thankfully, Josh is a rational human being.

"How did Levi seem to you?" Josh asks.

I can't get Levi out of my head, how intently he was listening to the people around him talking like he wasn't there. That fucking Dr. Pearson, basically sentencing him to life in an institution, right in front of him. It can't be easy to hear your doctor say you'll never grow up. Never be independent. Never be anything but a child needing constant supervision. Does all of that upset him?

"I don't know. Mostly normal, I guess. I was expecting . . . from the words they kept throwing around . . ."

I was expecting a stranger who belongs in an institution. Someone who is better off cloistered from the public. But he was just . . . himself. He was just the Levi I used to know. He was calm, stable, but he's locked up in there like he's a danger to the public. My little brother, the only person on Earth who's shared my experiences, had my childhood, knows my life.

Out of nowhere, tears well in my eyes and burn my throat. I try to disguise them with a cough but soon I'm quietly sobbing.

"Hey," Josh says softly. He squeezes my shoulder. "It's okay, Keira, go ahead and cry. This is a scary, confusing time. Crying is allowed."

"I just . . . don't know what's happening," I say, even though that's not quite what I mean.

"I know it's strange, seeing him in a place like that," he says. "We're doing the best thing possible for him right now."

"What, locking him up?"

"I mean putting him under the care of professionals. Getting him the medicine he needs."

I don't understand how all those drugs are supposed to help. Don't psychiatric drugs turn you into a zombie? I think of my silly Levi, noticing ceiling tiles and wanting me to tour Chernobyl, and think of him stripped of everything that makes him unique. I clench my fists. How is a forced emotional flatline supposed to make him better?

My little brother didn't want to live anymore.

I shove the tears out of my eyes.

"You okay?" Josh asks.

I nod as we pull up to our house on Evergreen Place. I see everything through the lens Levi must have had. He wanted to leave the cream-and-red craftsman-style house we grew up in. I go to the backyard and sit on the deck. He wanted to leave our fire pit. Our leaf-clogged trampoline. Our ancient, abandoned tree-house. I climb up the rope ladder and peek inside to see my old toy kitchen set and the plastic army guys he left up there years ago. He wanted to leave them, too.

The living room couch we both laid on during sick days. The dining room table, still full of marks from when we pounded our forks into the soft wood. The pictures on the walls and the plaques we make in memory of each pet that dies. He wanted to leave our current cats, Markie Mark and Snowball.

I wander into the front hall where, six years ago, we first met Josh. He was a twenty-six-year-old kid, almost scared of us. He gave me a CD of a band he thought I'd like (I did). He gave Levi a *Stones of Zendar* action figure. It's still in Levi's old toy bin in the basement, the package unopened.

He wanted to leave all of that.

And me. How could he want to leave me?

I've spent the past year working to save up for France, and the rest of my free time memorizing Jacques's daily schedule and inserting myself into it, determined to endear myself to him.

This is my wake-up call.

I go up to my room and sit on my bed, staring at the photos pinned to my wall. Big Ben. St. Petersburg's Winter Palace. The Eiffel Tower. Notre Dame. Versailles, where Marie Antoinette lived and breathed, where I've fantasized about finding a portal to go back in time and save her from the guillotine. Rivers and crowded streets and flags. Places I swear I'm going to find all the missing pieces of myself.

Levi and I have something in common. We both want to leave this place. The only difference is that I want to come back. I want to shepherd him out into the world, show him how beautiful it is, and come home again carrying sparks inside us. Maybe if he sees the world, sees everything it has to offer in a brand-new corner of it, he'll want to stay in it.

I want to take him there, and more importantly, bring him back.

And I have six thousand dollars to do it with.

# Chapter Four

For the past few years, I've had trouble with "balance" in my life. That's how the guidance counselor put it. Most people my age don't know the meaning of the word *moderation*—we binge-watch TV shows, stay up all night studying before exams, eat whole cartons of ice cream in one sitting—but I like to think I'm particularly good at over-doing stuff. When something feels good, I go at it full throttle. When something feels the slightest bit bad, I completely wipe it from my mind.

I first saw Jacques St-Pierre in my Global Stewardship club, on his first day in America. He looked like an elite European soccer player. He wore a button-down shirt tucked into gray trousers, with mahogany leather pointed dress shoes. His sleeves were rolled up to show off sculpted forearms. His hair blew upwards from his forehead, tousled but carefully engineered. Whenever anyone spoke to him, his eyebrow would slowly lift, as though evaluating every word they said. His evaluations ended, most often, in a smirk.

He was beautiful. He spoke French, the language I'd spent years teaching myself. He was from freaking *Versailles*. When he introduced himself to the Global Stewardship club, he said he was interested in art and philosophy. I was a puddle on the classroom floor from the moment he opened his mouth and said *"bonjour."* I was sure the custodians would have to come mop me up.

Jacques was . . . problematic. He would roll his eyes whenever most girls spoke to him. He would complain prodigiously about the school's food. He even complained about it when I organized a French Food Festival with the Culinary Arts class, entirely for his benefit. Our school had a daycare on campus, and he would snigger anytime he saw a student dropping off or picking up her baby, slinging a diaper bag alongside her backpack.

Oh, and he strung me along, using me for my car and my willingness to stroke his ego. I would've stroked more than that, too, and I wondered why he never asked me to. Until, of course, he told me I was *"trop grosse."*

It took me months to realize just how much of a douche he was. But my point is, for a long time, he felt good. I felt important, being at his side, being his own personal ambassador. Special, chosen. It's a cliché, but he was a drug and I was a junkie. I used him for the rush, and to escape.

Levi, the malevolent spirit haunting our house, did not feel good. I disengaged. I stayed disengaged right up until today, seeing him in the treatment center. Right up until now, I had been sure disengaging was best—I was protecting myself from all the bad shit. Protecting myself was good, wasn't it?

I wasn't protecting myself; I was blinding myself. I'm ready to fix that now.

When I first asked to sit down and talk with Mom and Josh, Mom had a million excuses. *I have to be with Levi, another doctor is coming. I promised I'd smuggle him McDonald's for dinner. He needs me to bring him fresh clothes.* I want to turn every word she's ever used on me around. Who's holding her emotions at arm's length now?

When she eventually finds a shred of time, Josh shuts off *Stones of Zendar,* and we all sit down at the dining room table in the dying sunlight.

"What's up, honey?" Mom asks. "What's that?"

I have a piece of paper in front of me, covered in my own scribbles, estimates, and calculations.

"I'll get to it." I tuck my hair behind my ear. My hand shakes so badly, my thumbnail scratches my cheek. "Um, so—"

"Is this about Levi?" Mom cuts me off. "Because you had the opportunity to ask Dr. Pearson lots of questions. Josh and I can try to answer them, but he's the expert. Why don't you come with me tomorrow and—"

"This isn't about Levi," I interrupt. "Well, it is. But not about medical stuff, or any of that."

"What's it about, Keira?" Josh asks. He tilts his head gently forward, nudging me to speak. I take a deep breath.

"You guys know how badly I want to go to Europe." I fold, unfold, and refold one corner of my paper. "And how I have the money to go, and all that stuff, right? Well, I was kind of wondering . . . if . . ."

God, this all sounds awful in my head right now. *Can I please kidnap your son and whisk him off across international waters?*

"I was wondering if I could ask Levi if he wants to come. If he doesn't want to, that's totally fine. But if he does . . . well, it might be really good for him. I have enough money, and he already has a passport, so . . ."

Josh nods slowly, like he's considering it fairly and rationally. But Mom leans forward and covers her face with her hands. "I can't believe this," she says. "Your brother's life is in danger and you're asking if you can take him to *Europe*? The best place for him to be is *here*, Keira. No, Josh, no, I'm not going to hear any different." She swats Josh's hand away. "Keira, I'm sorry we've inconvenienced you, but I really don't think Europe is a good idea for *anybody* right now."

"*Inconvenienced me?*" I repeat. "Do you think I just want to take him so I can go on my trip after all? How selfish do you think I am?"

"Okay, guys, calm down," Josh says. "Amanda, take a deep breath. That's not what Keira was implying."

"At *all*," I confirm.

"Keira." He gives me a look. "Think about this from your mom's perspective. She almost lost her son. Do you think she's going to be keen for him to leave right now?"

I blurt out, "Going to Europe isn't the same as dying."

I instantly regret it. Mom bursts into tears, her face folding and puckering and quivering, glaring at me like *look what you've done*.

"Keira," Josh tries again. "Why don't we talk about this later, when we all have level heads?"

I stand. "Don't bother. If you're not even going to try to listen, don't fucking bother."

I walk out, up the stairs, and to my room. My whole body quakes like a volcano threatening to erupt. I close my bedroom door and lean against it. Classic Mom. Jumping to conclusions and admitting what she really thinks of me. Uncaring. Selfish. Irresponsible. That's me, in Mom's eyes.

She almost lost a son, but I almost lost a brother. And that means *nothing* to her. She's blind to everyone's emotions but her own. She'll carry on about her disappointment but not even apologize for calling me a slut.

When they come, I almost choke on my tears. Classic Keira. Mini-breakdown alone in my room and then I'll cave and do everything Mom wants. Postpone the trip indefinitely so I can stew in the suburban hellhole that drove my brother crazy. The Eiffel Tower and the glittering gold of Versailles fade into nothingness in my mind. More tears bubble out and then I get mad.

I should be allowed to get mad. I want this *so bad*. I think about Levi in a hospital, cloistered and bored, and then I imagine him at my side in Paris, Amsterdam, Rome, seeing the things he always reads about in books and making me laugh until I pee like he used to when we were little. Mom used to worry that I had bladder problems because of how frequently Levi made me have accidents. God, it's been so long since he made me laugh like that.

I have to fight for that.

I'm about to go back downstairs to plead my case, grovel on my hands and knees if I have to, when there's a soft knock on my door.

"Keira?" It's Josh. "Want to come downstairs and we'll talk this over more civilly?"

"Can Mom agree to that?"

"She already has."

I open the door to his gentle smile. He leads me to the living room, where Mom has mopped up her face and sits with her favorite *Stones of Zendar* throw pillow in her lap.

"We still need to talk to Dr. Pearson of course," Josh says. "We can't say yes without permission from Levi's medical team. But we want to hear your side of this first."

"It's no secret that I've wanted to go for ages," I start. "But when I saw Levi today, I realized how far away I've gotten from him. I know you guys don't want me to go on the trip alone, so—"

"Do you think sending Levi off alone makes me feel better?" Mom asks.

"He wouldn't be alone, he'd be with me." I add *don't you trust me?* in my head but I don't dare say it.

"You heard Dr. Pearson today," Mom says. "Levi's not going to be able to drive, or live alone, or take care of himself without help. He's not like you. He's not going to college or—"

"Dr. Pearson doesn't know anything," I counter. "He talks about Levi like he's an inanimate object. And he sure as hell doesn't know me. Neither do you, Mom, remember?"

She glares daggers at me. "Don't you bring that up."

"What? The fact that you called me a slut this morning?"

"Keira!" Josh shouts.

"It's true, Josh, she literally said that."

"It's not my fault that you don't tell me anything." Mom crosses her arms over her chest. "How am I supposed to know every detail of your life if you don't tell me?"

"It doesn't matter—*you're not supposed to automatically assume I'm a whore!* I'm your child! Or do you forget that you have more than one of those?"

"Shh!" Josh cuts in. "Shh, everybody. Calm, remember?" He squeezes Mom's shoulder. "Why don't we ask Levi himself about all this tomorrow? Then we can see if he wants to go at all. Why don't we let his wishes guide this?"

Mom nods. "We might not even need to have this discussion at all."

"Well, we'll let Levi decide," Josh corrects her.

Mom stands and goes to the kitchen, where she starts dinner, pots and pans banging together more than necessary. Josh catches me on my way back upstairs and gives me a smile.

"I'll keep working on her," he says. "I promise I'll get her to consider this fairly. I think it's a great idea, and I know it comes from a good place."

I search his face to make sure he's telling the truth. I can't tell for sure, but he wants me to feel comforted, and that's more than I can say for my biological parent.

"Thanks, Josh."

"No problem, kid. Love you."

"Love you, too."

For the hundred thousandth time, I thank the god of stepfathers for sending Josh.

# CHAPTER FIVE

Mom and Josh go to the treatment center gift shop, saying they needed to buy Levi some cough drops, and I go up to his room. He's watching cartoons with an irritated frown, ignoring the nurse trying to get him to take a cup of pills.

"Come on, Levi. You know you have to. I'm not going away until you take these." She turns when she hears my shoes on the linoleum. "Oh, this must be your sister. Here for a visit?"

I smile. "Yup. Hi, Lev."

He grunts and finally reaches for the pills, downing them without the glass of water the nurse hands him. She makes him open his mouth and lift his tongue before she walks away, satisfied.

I sit down next to his bed. "How's it going today?"

"Good. *Looney Tunes* is on. With Road Runner."

"Oh, cool." I turn to the TV and we watch for a few minutes. "Remember watching these cartoons at Grandma's when we were little?"

Before I started my job at Safeway, Mom would drag us to her parents' house every Sunday. Grandma and Grandpa made French toast with sticky syrup, blueberry pancakes, and the greasiest sausages imaginable. Levi and I would watch cartoons, eating our breakfast off those wooden TV trays old people always seem to have. We'd fight the whole time—over the pancakes with the

most blueberries, the crispiest bacon, *Looney Tunes* or *Scooby-Doo.*
Mom would always turn from the adults' conversation and snap
at me to let Levi have his way. *Looney Tunes* was fine, since Levi
liked it so much. But there were so many Sundays I was dying to
know what Scooby and the gang were up to on the other channel.

"Hmm," Levi says. "Are Mom and Josh here?"

"In the shop."

He grunts.

"Hey, Lev . . . I have a question for you."

"What."

"You know about my trip."

"Yeah."

"I was wondering if you wanted to come. We could make it
smaller if you don't want to go all over Europe, maybe just France.
What do you think?"

He looks at me. Well, not at me. But his eyes are fixed on
some point on my face, kind of near my chin. "Come to France
with you?"

"Yeah."

"Hmm." He looks back at the TV and purses his lips, sliding them back and forth across his teeth. "Do you have enough
money?"

My heart starts to beat a little harder. If he was totally unin-
terested, he would ignore me or tell me to fuck off.

"Yeah."

His fingers with their bitten-down nails start to pick at his
blanket. He pulls it over his lap and frowns as he arranges it just
so. When it's tucked around his feet, he pats it all down. He looks
like a caterpillar making its cocoon.

"Did Mom say it's okay?"

"She's . . . not thrilled. I think Josh is on board. They want to
ask the doctors what they think, though."

"The doctors might say no."

"Yeah, maybe."

A second passes, then two, then three, then . . .

"We should go. Soon. Preferably two days after I get home."

"Yeah?" I try to control my smile. "So I should buy our plane tickets, then? We'll fly to Paris?"

He nods and scratches his nose.

Paris. After all this time, *Paris*.

"Okay, so," Levi says. His voice is relatively light. Still monotone, but he sounds almost content. "I'll probably come home in a week. You should buy the tickets for the twenty-fifth."

"Okay."

Mom and Josh come up then and we spend the afternoon watching TV and laughing, Levi pointing out the many things he finds ridiculous. I can barely concentrate. Paris and possibilities burn a hole in me.

In the car on the way home, I break the news.

"He said yes!" I say, trying to rein in my excitement. "He wants to come to Paris! He wants to leave on the twenty-fifth!"

Josh smiles. "He actually wants to? That's great!"

"I know, I can't believe it."

Mom says nothing. Her eyebrows furrow in the rearview mirror. She really looks her age when she's worried. Forty-five. Josh could be the son she had in high school instead of her husband.

We pull into the driveway at home, and when Josh gets out of the car and we're alone, she asks, "Does he *really* want to go?"

"You know how stubborn he is. If he didn't want to go, he wouldn't even talk about it."

"You aren't bending Levi to your will, are you?" she whispers, looking down into her lap.

Resisting the urge to freak out, I measure my words with a teaspoon. "No, Mom. I wouldn't do that."

She lets out the longest sigh in the world. "We have to consult Dr. Pearson," she says. "But if it's what Levi wants . . . maybe we can find a way."

And it is. It is, it is, it is.

# CHAPTER SIX

While Mom meets with Dr. Pearson, I wander the house all day, wringing my hands. When she gets home, she slams the front door and shouts, "Dr. Pearson gives the green light!" before kicking off her shoes and stomping to the kitchen.

I do a happy dance in my room, and once I'm calm, I spend the night stepping up my plane ticket research game.

Levi comes home three days later, but his plan to leave for Paris exactly two days after returning home is dashed. Mom insists that we spend two weeks at home before leaving. On Levi's first night back, I sit with him in his room and he complains, "Two weeks of dealing with Mom. Yay, exactly what I wanted."

"She's just worried about you," I tell him.

He grunts and plays with the hospital wristband he's still wearing.

"At least we have Josh on our side," I say. "He's a lot more rational than Mom."

"Because he's not our dad," Levi says.

"Come on. He is our dad by this point."

"He isn't our blood."

Every couple years, we have this argument. It's always the same.

"Blood means nothing. Josh acts like a better dad than our real father ever did, even when he was around. That counts for more."

Levi shakes his head. "No blood relation. Not our dad."

I roll my eyes. I *hate* when Levi talks like this. He always favors the guy who walked out on us over the guy who walked in, sat down, and stayed. It's not fair. I give our birth father exactly what he deserves: nothing, not so much as a thought. I've worshiped Josh since the first time he cooked us mac and cheese with cut-up hot dogs in it, but Levi barely speaks to him. I once had a nightmare where Josh heard Levi say he hates him. I woke up in tears.

Our huge, fat, white cat, aptly named Snowball, waltzes into Levi's room and plants himself in my lap. He looks up at me like "what are you going to do about it?" Levi chuckles and slides off his bed. He shuffles closer to me and pats Snowball's head.

"I wish we could bring Snowball to Paris," Levi murmurs.

I hear that for what it is: *I hope the trip will be okay.*

"It'll be fine, Levi," I tell him.

He grunts.

The two weeks at home, I quickly learn, are so Mom can let me know just how much she doesn't trust me. I'm eating breakfast one day when she walks in, shuffling a stack of index cards.

"What are those?" I ask, slurping my cereal milk.

She holds the first one up in response. There's a picture of a small, white pill, and the words ONE PILL, TWICE DAILY.

"They're flash cards," Mom says. "With all of Levi's medication on them."

I manage to refrain from rolling my eyes. "You couldn't just tell me all this? You had to make flash cards?"

"This is how you learn," she says, flipping to the next card: red pill, ONE PILL, THREE TIMES DAILY WITH FOOD. "This is no different from your times tables."

"You don't think it's a little condescending?" I point out. "Seeing as I'm eighteen, not eight?"

She says, "Until you can recite all this information, you're not going on your trip. I need to trust that you can take care of Levi."

"You could just give me a list."

She shakes her head and flips to the next card. "You need to know this backwards and forwards."

I knew she was right—of course I needed to know Levi's meds schedule, I was the adult on the trip—but she flipped the cards so aggressively, holding them right in my face. I had to grit my teeth and bite my tongue, but I eventually played along.

It only took a few minutes before I could tell you how many of the blue pills Levi needed every day, and whether or not he needed to take the orange capsules with food, but Mom ran me through the flashcards every day leading up to our departure. She wrote me a final test a few days before we left.

"See, I was right," Mom said when I passed that test with flying colors. "You *do* learn best with flash cards."

◌◌◌ ◌◌◌

The night before we leave, Mom pops her head into the bathroom while I'm dabbing a clay mask on my face.

"We don't want you to get arrested for kidnapping," Mom says, presenting me with an envelope, "so I wrote you a letter of parental consent to travel as his guardian."

Wow, thanks for not wanting me to get arrested and charged with a felony, Mom. But I manage to accept the envelope with a smile.

"But this isn't just a free-for-all," she says before launching into stuff she's repeated hundreds of times this week. "We want you to be in constant contact. Text us *every day* with that app Josh made you download. Every day, got it?"

I nod. "Got it."

"Tell us every little thing about how Levi's feeling. And . . ." She takes a deep breath. "Keira, it's your obligation to make sure he's taking his medications. If anything, anything at all, goes wrong . . ."

She's all but telling me it'll be my fault. I want to reply with a metric ton of sarcasm—*"Nooooo, Mom, I'm going to make sure he gets super depressed and jumps into the Seine!"*

"Of course," is all I say.

"And," Mom continues. She holds out a folded piece of notebook paper. It trembles in her hand. "I want you to have a look at this. It's—it's Levi's note."

His suicide note? I stare at the little slip of paper. It looks so innocent, but who knows what could be written there?

"No," I splutter. "No, Mom, I can't. I don't want to know what it says."

She still holds it out to me. "I really think you should."

What could he have said when he thought he was about to die? Our last interaction before he wrote that letter was horrid—what if he mentioned it? There's no way I can read anything he could say about that. Why would she push this on me at the last minute? Is she trying to scare me? To make me change my mind about the trip? If that's her goal, if she's using fear to manipulate me into doing what she wants . . . that's a new low.

"No, Mom," I whisper. "I can't."

She exhales loudly, flaring her nostrils. She retracts the note, pulling it in close to her body. "Fine."

It's not fine. My heart pounds as I wash off my face mask; panic prickles at the edges of my vision as I stare myself down in the mirror. I completely lost my chill. Did Mom want me to be so distraught I'd call off the trip and check myself into Levi's treatment center? Does she hate me that much?

Our flight leaves at 11:30 a.m. on a bright, sunny Tuesday. I wake up at six; I couldn't possible sleep any more. I shower, dress, all the while thinking *in a matter of hours, I'll be in Paris* and internally freaking out. Levi wakes early, too, packing last-minute things into his suitcase. Extra pairs of socks, his iPod, his alarm clock.

"Why are you bringing that?"

"So we'll wake up?" Levi says with a *duh* kind of tone.

"The hostel will have alarm clocks, y'know. Cell phones have alarm clocks."

He zips up the suitcase, alarm clock still inside. "I would rather have my own clock so I know for sure how to use it."

I smile secretly. "Okay, whatever. Ready to go?"

He nods.

Mom stays out of our way as we lug our suitcases downstairs and out to Josh's car. We've arranged this: Josh will drive us to the airport, and Mom will say good-bye at home, to minimize her stress. And mine.

When we're ready, she hugs me for like three seconds and clings to Levi for what feels like hours. After patting her back once, he just stands there awkwardly.

"Be safe," she whispers when she finally pulls back.

I swallow my sarcasm, smile, and wave.

It's a forty-minute drive to the airport, through downtown Seattle. I'm nervous like I've never been nervous before. The song on the radio is too fast; it sets a bad example for my heartbeat.

We're actually on our way. *Paris*, the city of my heart! And I'm going there without Jacques. I never thought I would've been happy about that, but I close my eyes for a few seconds and imagine what it would really be like to have Jacques in the back seat right now instead of Levi. I would have painstakingly loaded up my face with makeup this morning, and subsequently worried about it staying pristine, even on the transatlantic flight. I probably would have bought an entirely new wardrobe for the trip—told myself I'd compromise on souvenirs and experiences in Paris to balance out the money I was blowing on clothes. I would spend the whole trip worrying about how I looked or reining in my excitement to match Jacques's cool detachment.

No, thank you. Without him, I can be comfortable, practical, and I can be myself. I can safely geek out with Levi; he wouldn't judge me or laugh at me. I mean, no more than he usually does. He is my little brother, after all.

I glance at him in the backseat. He's gazing out the window, eyes actually shining.

"Excited, Levi?" I ask him.

He nods and scratches his nose, his face scrunched up. I go back to quietly freaking out.

Finally, we arrive at SeaTac. Josh pulls the car to the curb at Departures like I tell him to.

"Are you sure you don't want me to park and walk you guys inside?" Josh asks.

"No, it's okay." I flash a quick smile. "We'll be fine, Josh."

I'm partially saying it to reassure myself, but apparently I convinced him. He gives me a quick hug. Levi climbs out of the car without a word of good-bye.

"Good luck," Josh says. "You guys will be fine, I know it."

I can't speak around the lump in my throat. I just nod. We unload our suitcases and Josh gives us a wave before he drives away, disappearing into the airport traffic.

Then it's just me and Levi against the world.

We're stupid early. Our flight isn't even on the board yet, so we sit in the banks of plastic seats and . . . do nothing. Levi stares at the floor, where he taps his taps his rubber boots incessantly. I look everywhere else. We face this huge, massive wall of check-in stations, where people are being greeted by overly friendly airline representatives and having their luggage weighed before they walk off into the Great Beyond. Or someplace.

"Want to go check out the shops?" I ask, pointing down the long row of storefronts. "Looks like they have books and magazines and stuff."

Levi shakes his head. A tiny crease appears between his eyebrows.

"What do you want to do?"

"Just sit."

"Why don't we walk around or something?"

"No, Keira, God . . ."

"Okay, jeez! Forgive me."

"*You* can go walk around."

"I don't want to go by myself!"

He gives the most exaggerated eye roll I've ever seen.

"Fine," I snap. "Watch my suitcase."

My feet carry me down the line of shops, but none of them interests me anymore. I wanted to look through them with Levi. I wanted to laugh at the creepy stuffed anthropomorphic Space Needles, to pick out a dumb magazine like *Trucker's Monthly* and read it together. I wanted us to read the backs of crappy romance novels using our dramatic movie trailer voices. Once we spent hours in Walmart, Levi deadpanning titles like *A Man for Keeps* and *Her Wild Cowboy*, and I laughed so hard that, like the old days, I peed. Luckily, Walmart sells underwear.

That was . . . God, almost two years ago.

I glance over my shoulder. Levi's tousled head looks up at the ceiling and down to the floor, turns sideways as he scratches his nose. He seems so small from here. He looks so lost.

I dart inside the newsagent's, buying two Cokes and the silliest romance novel on the shelf.

"Here." I pass him his Coke as I sit next to him. "I got you a little reading material for the plane."

His eyes lose a bit of their glassiness when he sees the book cover. Two wind-blown models stare at each other lustily, the man pushing the woman up against a horse.

"*The Billionaire Rancher's Bride*," he reads. His lips twist. "I like his chaps."

As our wait stretches on, his monotone becomes a little less—well, monotonous. If I were to draw a Levi Mood Map, the level would be steadily rising. He nudges me and points out a tiny dog in a tiny carrier. A typo on a passerby's Star Wars T-shirt (DARTH VADER WANT'S YOU) makes him laugh out loud.

The best is an old lady in brand-new, ultra-hip Nikes, the b-baller kind with neon colors.

"She's trying to be down with us hip kids," Levi murmurs. "In her muumuu and fur coat."

I fail at not-laughing. "Don't make fun! She—she probably got them as a gift or something."

"I bet they help her get money and hoes."

"*Levi!*"

His smile turns smug and he starts to fade back into monotone Levi, slumping against the chair and kicking his legs. The line on that mood chart is dropping, so I cast my eye about for something to boost him. He's going to back out. Get scared.

"Our flight's on the board!" I cry, pointing. "Paris, flight 905, at 11:38! We can check in now."

"I have to go to the bathroom," he says.

Two hours is loads of time, but somehow it seems like it could all tick away in the few minutes it takes to go to the bathroom.

I use the women's bathroom and then wait for Levi outside the men's. It's a bit weird that it isn't him waiting for me. I've walked out of countless mall or movie theatre bathrooms to see him dragging his feet as he paces the floor, excruciatingly bored. A quick glance around tells me he's definitely still inside.

I wait.

I fish my cell phone out of my pocket and keep an eye on the time. One hour and fifty minutes until our flight leaves. Where the hell is Levi?

Another few minutes go by. My scalp starts to prickle and I'm ready to charge into the bathroom to find him, because this is not normal. Levi does not disappear, and he does not get chatty or comfortable in bathrooms. He gets in and gets right out, after washing his hands at least twice. What if something's wrong in there?

I'm about to really panic when Levi finally meanders languidly out of the bathroom.

"What took you so long? Jeez, I was freaking out!"

"Calm down, *God*." His forehead twitches in annoyance. "I was just looking at the tiles."

"What?"

"The tiles in the bathroom. The workmanship is pretty good. I'm impressed."

I can't think of a thing to say. I had forgotten he was such a weirdo. Who admires bathroom tiles for ten minutes?

This bodes well. If he likes examining tiles in minute detail, he'll love the Louvre.

I drag my tile-admiring brother to check-in, take out our passports, check our luggage, and walk through to the Great Beyond. It feels amazing to just have my backpack, no more giant suitcase to tow around. Wait . . .

"Levi, you don't have any carry-on luggage?"

Levi is just standing there, hands in his hoodie pouch, completely un-weighed down. I have a backpack full of stuff for the long flight. Levi has . . . nothing.

His dull eyes suddenly sharpen.

"Our luggage goes away?"

"Yeah, it goes into the luggage compartment, underneath the plane."

"We can't get stuff out of it?"

"No, not now that it's gone!"

He blinks three times and his lower lip slips out.

"My iPod was in there," he murmurs. "And my book."

I groan. "Levi, what were you thinking?"

"I didn't know, okay?" He glares, but his cheeks start to redden.

He isn't the one who did all the travel research, I realize. He hasn't been scouring the Internet for tips on what to bring and how to pack. He's naive, an embarrassed kid who now has nothing to do on a ten-hour flight. The urge to protect him flares up inside of me, even from something as harmless as boredom. But boredom isn't always harmless, especially to Levi. Ten hours with only in-flight entertainment, which he's guaranteed to hate and sneer at? I don't even want to think about what could go on in his head if he's sitting there, unoccupied and stewing, for ten hours. And I'll have to sit there and apologize to everyone who will give us the evil eye over his groans and kicking legs—if he can even move his legs in a cramped airplane seat. I'll look like an incompetent babysitter.

I flash back to Dr. Pearson, saying Levi would never be a functioning adult. I think this is the kind of thing he meant.

"I'm sorry, Lev," I say.

He grunts and turns to walk toward security.

I offer to buy him a new book in the shops on the other side of security. I offer to buy him video game magazines, the latest Stephen King novel, anything he wants. He refuses it all.

Then I notice *The Billionaire Rancher's Bride,* tucked into his hoodie pocket, his hand curled around it. We board the plane, shuffling around all the dads in vacation attire trying to stuff bags into the overheard compartments, and when we finally locate our seats, Levi pulls out *The Billionaire Rancher's Bride* and starts to read.

It feels like I get a chance to peek behind the curtain and see the little child pulling the levers behind Levi's cynical exterior. Innocence and earnestness, eagerly turning pages when he thinks I'm not looking. This is the real Levi.

# CHAPTER SEVEN

I've always fantasized about finding love on an airplane. A sexy stranger would be seated across the aisle. A boy a few years older than me, French or British or Norwegian. Maybe a college student, or a guy taking a gap year and doing nothing but wandering. A guy with interesting stories to tell and passions to share, like scuba diving or mountain climbing or basket-weaving. I don't know. Anything. We'll connect like in a nineties romantic comedy, like Meg Ryan and Tom Hanks.

That doesn't happen this time. I keep my eyes peeled for any kind of promise, but the other passengers prove to be hopelessly mundane. I occupy myself with a book, music, podcast rotation. Levi finishes *The Billionaire Rancher's Bride* and when I ask him how it was, he says, "Pretty good. Although I don't think there's really that much money in ranching." To my infinite relief, he falls asleep after that. He spends the rest of the flight snoring and twitching beside me.

When the countdown to arrival hits thirty minutes and my ears pop with the dropping altitude, people open their window shades and peer outside. It's so bright it's like we're landing on the sun. The light reveals countryside below, dotted with towns and a few lakes and rivers. The country fades into more and more towns. French suburbia, I guess.

And then, suddenly, I recognize shapes and outlines I've seen a hundred times on maps. The twist of a river or the shape of a town gives me déjà vu. Paris. It's out there.

It takes forever and a half for the plane to land. A million adjustments and realignments and shuffling back and forth before we're finally safe at our gate. Then, after standing up and joining the jostling queue, it takes another half of forever to disembark. Levi, all disoriented after his nap, tenses up. His shoulders hunch, his eyes start to dart around, looking for an escape.

We finally snake our way off the plane. We're free, turned loose in Charles de Gaulle Airport.

I've given up my expectation of finding love on an airplane, but I'm still open to a baggage claim meet-cute. Levi's suitcase came along the carousel right away, but as we wait for mine, I look around, hunting for cute hair, cute legs in cute jeans, adorable smiles . . .

I spot an artful haircut and spindly legs and my interest is piqued, but when his head turns, I freeze.

Jacques.

Jacques St-Pierre. A hundred feet away, his arm around Selena Henderson's waist. Wait, did Selena dye her hair black?

Then Jacques grins, and his eyes crinkle and he laughs, and that is so not Jacques. It could be his twin, but it's not him. That girl is not Selena.

All the air comes rushing out of my lungs in relief, but I can't stop staring at this totally random couple. What if Selena did come back to France with Jacques to stay at his row house in Versailles? What if the two of them exchanged sloppy kisses at the baggage carousel, exactly like these two?

The thought brings tears to my eyes, for Past Me's sake. Present Me doesn't want Jacques, doesn't give a rat's ass about him—but like she's my heartbroken friend, I sympathize with Past Me. These doppelgängers look so happy, and seeing them hurts Past Me. That was supposed to be her happily ever after. Poor girl.

"Keira, I think that's your bag," Levi says. "Keira? Keira, get your bag."

Levi shuffles pigeon-toed alongside the carousel, rubber boots squeaking on the floor. He grabs the suitcase and hauls it off, whacking some lady in the butt.

"Ouch!" she yelps.

"Levi!" I hiss. "I'm so sorry, ma'am!"

She glares at Levi, who has already yanked up the handle on my suitcase and is now dragging both our bags over to stare intently at a wall rack full of brochures with titles like *What to do now that you're in Paris?* and *Day trips to die for!*

I glance over my shoulder to see that Fake Jacques and Quasi-Selena have found their bags. They're walking up the concourse with them, fingers entwined. They get on a moving sidewalk and gaze into each other's eyes. They can actually speak to each other; how the hell do Jacques and Selena communicate? Selena used to always get the verbs "avoir" and "être" mixed up in study group, saying "*je suis fini*" instead of "*j'ai fini*" when we finished assignments— saying she was dead, instead of finished. And Jacques's English is far from amazing. Do they communicate entirely through tracing the shapes of letters with their tongues while they kiss?

I turn away from them and the trip to France I always dreamed of. I focus on the trip I have, which is Levi roughly grabbing brochures and creasing them with his grubby hands.

"What are we doing first?" he asks.

"I dunno," I mutter.

"Hey, *Museums of Paris*. Looks like there are some war museums."

Thank God world peace hasn't happened yet. Levi would be bored to tears.

"Yeah," I say. "We should definitely check those out."

Levi grunts approvingly. He's visibly better than he was even a few minutes ago. He's standing up taller, his arms move more freely, and he's even *smiling* a bit.

I fire off a quick text to Mom via TextAnywhere, the free international messaging app Josh made me download: *Landed in Paris, Mom! Everything's fine!*

Well, except for having my heart stomped on in front of me.

Her reply is just a single word: *Great.*

I sigh.

I pre-booked tickets for a shuttle bus into the city, so we go outside to the pickup loop. It's full of taxis and double-deckers. My heart flutters. I've never been on a double-decker.

"Um, *excusez-moi*," I say to the driver, who's leaning against the side of the big, white double-decker with, I think, the right logo. "*Est-ce que nous sommes dans la correcte place?*"

His eyes crinkle. Is he laughing at my stupid American accent? But he looks at our tickets, says, "*Oui, mademoiselle*," and helps us load our luggage under the bus as we climb aboard.

I lead us to the itty-bitty staircase leading to the second level. Levi grabs the back of my shirt. "Not up there."

"But I've never been on a double-decker before!"

"I'm sure it's exactly the fucking same as a regular bus. Come on, let's sit down here."

I keep climbing. "You can if you want."

There's a pair of old people in Hawaiian shirts and a handful of Asian schoolgirls sitting up here, but somehow, the seats at the very front are empty. I hurry toward them and sit where it feels like I'm teetering on the edge above the road.

Levi's great weight plonks down beside me. His jacket rustles. He sighs.

"This is so cool, right?" I say, grasping the handrail in front of us.

He grunts begrudgingly.

I thought the bus was cool at a standstill, but when it starts to move, it blows my mind. Without seeing the driver, it feels like the bus magically pulls itself into traffic. We bounce and sway like crazy, and when we stop, it seems like we're going to slide over the top of the cars in front of us.

"This is giving me a headache," Levi says once we're on a highway, tiny little cars zipping along around us.

"So close your eyes."

He does, and within seconds, Levi's head has fallen back and he's snoring. I get my first glimpses of Paris alone.

So far, it looks like the outskirts of any other city: industrial. The names of cosmetic companies plaster the sides of giant warehouses and clinical-looking facilities. You'd picture *L'Oréal Paris* as swanky offices with views of the Arc de Triomphe, not blocky, slate-gray buildings that look the same as they would in Hicktown, USA. *This* is Paris?

And then I see it. Way off in the distance, almost fading into the cloudy sky, taller than anything else.

The Eiffel Tower. Just jutting out of the landscape, signaling to me. *You're here.*

I sit up and crane my neck, watching it for as long as I can before we drive between taller buildings and lose sight. It feels impossible, like the moment in *Jurassic Park* when they first see dinosaurs. That's *it*. That's the Eiffel Tower, that's my dream, off in the distance.

I'm here. With Levi beside me, I'm finally here.

# CHAPTER EIGHT

"I thought they drove on the other side of the road here," Levi says, blinking sleepily.

The bus has finally carried us into Paris proper. We navigate narrow streets lined with trees, a café on every corner.

"No, that's England."

"I'm pretty sure it was France."

"Well, obviously not, weirdo."

"Hmm." Levi stares out the window at the somewhat dingy shops we're passing. "Look, McDonald's. I could go for that."

"Look at all the cafés, though, Lev. Wouldn't you rather have lunch at a real Parisian café?"

"Not the ones here, Keira. They're all crappy."

I roll my eyes. Sure, maybe they have dirty awnings and garish neon signs, but still. Parisian café trumps McDonald's any day.

The bus finally slows and starts to turn into the Gare de l'Est. It's a squat, sprawling white building full of windows with a sun motif. It wouldn't be out of place on a Riviera near the Mediterranean. We disembark from the bus in a slow, long lineup of tourists—old people already clutching their cameras and mispronouncing French words.

"The Gare de l'Est is a lot more beautiful than I expected it to be," a woman just ahead of us says, snapping a picture through the bus window as we wait to climb down the stairs—only she pronounces it "jerr de least."

"It is, isn't it, Martha?" her friend muses. "But if you think this is beautiful, wait until you see Ver-sales tomorrow!"

Ver-sales! I want to freak out at them. *Gah-re de lest*, lady! *Vehr-sai!* Roll your r's. Skip the s's. Come on.

You should have to pass a test to be able to come here. You should have to prove you deserve it.

We grab our luggage and a wave of fatigue hits me. It's the middle of the night, according to my body, but it's barely nine o'clock in the morning here and I have to hold on. At least until a late-afternoon nap. We enter the big, noisy train station.

"So?" Levi says, looking up at the glass ceiling. "Where now?"

"To the hostel to drop off our stuff. It's in the *cinquième arrondissement*."

"What?"

"The fifth *arrondissement*," I repeat. "*Arrondissement* is like . . . rounding? Estimation? The different areas and neighborhoods of Paris are called *arrondissements*. There are twenty of them."

"Why don't you just call it the fifth neighborhood?" Levi grumbles.

"Because it's an *arrondissement*."

"God, you're so annoying."

"*I'm* annoying?"

He glares at me. "You keep trying to act like you're French, like it makes you better or something. Guess what, I don't *care*. Just be fucking normal."

My cheeks burn. As much as I hate to admit it . . . maybe I do sprinkle in random French words when they aren't absolutely necessary. Oh God, how dumb must I sound, saying "*bon matin*" in the morning or shouting "*bonne nuit*" down the hall before I go to bed. I just love the way they sound. Okay, and the way they make me sound. Except for the first day of senior year, when I volunteered to take Jacques to his next class and said *"bienvenue à notre école"*—before I'd learned exactly how to pronounce the accents. *Bienvenue ay notre ee-cole.* Oh God, it still hurts to remember his cruel laugh.

Levi's right about another thing: he doesn't care. With Levi, none of that posturing and posing matters. With Jacques, I was constantly performing. Eat a hot dog at lunch, he'd raise his eyebrows. The next day I'd nibble on a salad. I would have rather gone hungry than seen that dismissive look on his face when he looked at me. Now I can relax, be myself. I don't have to constantly try to impress someone who thinks he's slumming it with a chubby girl. *"Trop grosse."* Screw him.

I wonder if Selena is going through that song and dance. She's welcome to it.

I snap out of it and lead Levi down the stairs to the underground subway station. We head to a giant map of the metro system and my heart does this weird squish thing. Colored lines snake all over the page and trace a vague approximation of the city's shape and I'm proud of myself for recognizing it. I could stand here for ages, just reading the pretty names of all the stops and imagining the amazing places they could take me: *Quatre Septembres, Château d'Eau,* and, funnily enough, *Franklin D. Roosevelt.* Levi points that one out.

"Weird," he says. "We have to go there. Let's go there now."

"First we have to find the hostel. It's, um . . ." I pull out my street map of Paris and find the address I scrawled there. I find the stop nearest to it. "The nearest metro stop is Jussieu, I think. Right?"

"Why the hell are you asking me?"

The metro isn't as crowded as I imagined it, but it's just as full of Parisians. I mean, obviously. But not the Parisians of artwork and movies, with striped shirts and berets. They're business people. Students clutching textbooks, earbuds in and staring into space, biting the insides of their cheeks. Flustered-looking, but still immaculately put-together moms with small children.

We step back out into the morning sunshine at Jussieu, in a wide garden-like square opposite a university.

"*L'Université de Pierre et Marie Curie*," I read off a sign. "Oh my God, I should go to college here."

I can picture myself speed-walking across the campus, worrying about classes but also planning my fabulous Parisian social life. I'd be a sophisticated student, going to art museums and wine tastings on the weekend, not some sorority chick who cheers for the Tigers.

"No way," Levi says.

"Why not?"

"It's dumb." He falls in line behind me as I dart to the nearest crosswalk. I head toward the Seine. I know just where it is.

"If I like it here, wouldn't it be as good a place as any to study?"

Levi doesn't say anything as we weave our suitcases through a huge crowd of people. When we're able to walk side-by-side again, he says, "Everyone would just laugh at you because you're American."

Anger flares inside me for a moment, before I wonder if he's just saying that because he would miss me. I remember Dr. Trash Bag—I mean, Dr. Pearson—saying Levi needed to develop more effective communication skills, and now I know what he meant. Anger, insults, and condescension are not ways you should tell people you love them. Neither is shoving your sister into the mantelpiece on prom night.

We wander up the street in the direction I know is right. I've memorized all the maps, swallowed them whole. I instinctively know to cross the street here, to take the right fork in the road. We're on the street that borders the Seine. The city's islands are *right there*. The Ile de Saint-Louis, with its pretty, funny, old apartment buildings, and the place of Paris's genesis, the Ile de la Cité. Visible above the tops of the trees that line our street, the spire and towers of Notre Dame reach for the sky.

And the river itself is *right there*, the water Joan of Arc's ashes were spilled into. The river I've dreamed of rescuing her from— but I suppose the water was less cruel than the fire.

"Come on," I say to Levi, tugging my suitcase after me. "I want to see better. I *need* to see better."

"*Keira . . .*"

I rush to the nearest crosswalk. My wheels get stuck in a crack in the sidewalk and the suitcase nearly yanks my arm off. I don't care, though. I drag it along behind me, on a mission.

I reach that distant sidewalk and throw myself at the railing. The river sends a cool breeze to kiss my face and play with my hair. There it is. Notre Dame. The bold stone edifice dominates the landscape. The towers face away from us so all I can see is the arcing stone buttresses and the grand roof and the impossibly high, spiked spire. It's hard to believe something so beautiful and so much larger than life was built by human hands, centuries ago. I think of our house, with its flimsy, crumbling siding, barely twenty years old. The world is different now.

"Isn't it amazing?" I whisper to Levi. Coppery river air fills my mouth.

He doesn't say anything. I want to look at him and figure out what he's thinking, but it might break the spell. His hand is next to mine on the grimy rail, broad and meaty with surprisingly tiny fingernails, his wrist just resting while my hands clutch.

"So when do the gargoyles come to life and start singing?" he finally asks. His lips twist in a tiny smile.

"I think Disney took some artistic license there," I say, laughing.

"Some?"

"Okay, a lot."

"Did you know that in the book, Esmeralda is killed and Quasimodo lays beside her corpse in despair until he starves to death?"

"How did you know that? Have you read it?"

I've never read the book; always wanted to, but I'm scared to try. Levi, reading French literature? I imagine him curled up in his basement bedroom reading it and it makes me smile. Maybe we should take a Victor Hugo–themed walking tour or something.

"No," he mutters, frowning again. "I just read the plot summary on Wikipedia."

Oh.

"Is that the place we're staying?" Levi asks.

I glance over my shoulder. He points at a sandwich board–style sign across the street, outside a big wooden door propped open with a rock. It's the same white stone apartment building I spent so long gazing at online.

"Yes," I breathe, finally turning away from Notre Dame. I crane my neck to see the top floor windows. If we stay up there, I'll have an even better view of the towers and spires and the entire right bank of Paris.

We make our way back across the street. The weight of my suitcase is painful; I understand backpacking now. Maybe we can pick out the necessities, ship everything else back home, and buy a pair of outdoorsy-looking backpacks like the ones the people making their way into the hostel ahead of us have.

Right away, stepping in the door, I smell pot. It's faint, but definitely *there*, especially in the blissed-out smiles of two guys sitting on cushions in the living room–style lobby, reading art books.

Levi smells it, too. His body goes rigid. "Keira. We can't stay here."

The backpackers in front of us thank the ponytailed man behind the counter and head for the stairs.

"What are you talking about?" I whisper.

"It's dirty." His hands clench in and out of fists. "I can feel it."

"I've looked at pictures of the rooms online, Levi. It's *fine*."

"What can you tell from *pictures*? I'm not staying here."

The ponytail guy turns to us and smiles.

"*Bonjour!*" I say brightly. "*Je m'appelle Keira Braidwood, j'ai une reservation pour deux?*"

"Ah, *oui*." He shuffles some pages on a giant notepad calendar in front of him. "You will be in the *Salle de Versailles*. All the way up the stairs."

The Versailles Room. Like it's meant to be. Like Marie Antoinette herself is watching over us.

"Did you hear that, Levi? The Versailles Room!"

I whip my head around to look at him, but he's gone. His suitcase stands alone beside mine.

"Levi?" I look back at the ponytail guy. "Did you see where he went?"

The guy shrugs halfheartedly. Like it doesn't even matter.

"*Excusez-moi*," I say, grabbing both of the suitcases and rushing for the door.

He's standing just outside, facing the Seine, edging farther away from some German-speaking backpackers consulting a map. His fists wedge in tight against his chest, making his arms look like little bird wings.

"Levi, what's up?"

He frowns. "Don't want to stay there."

I look up at the windows of the Versailles Room. I picture a tall-ceilinged room full of dazzling light that spills in through a wall dominated by windows. Gilded ceiling, fantastically ornate crown moldings. An expensive portrait or two. All I can see is the white façade full of ordinary panes, with a plain, flat white ceiling beyond.

I sigh. "Why not?"

"Dirty."

"That's it?"

"I don't want to talk to *them*." He glares at the backpackers a few feet away. "Why can't we just stay in a regular hotel? Just us?"

"That's more expensive, Levi," I say, thinking of my bank account, imaginary numbers in an Internet browser that somehow rule my whole life.

"Can't we just find a cheap hotel? Please?"

"A cheap hotel would probably be worse than a good hostel. And if I spend more money, we'll have less money to do cool things or go to cool places."

He shrugs. His eyes search the street in front of us. He glances up at the staggering height of Notre Dame's spire. "Why do we have to do things?" he asks. "Can't we enjoy just being here?"

I swallow again. He's right, of course; we are in *Paris*, and any time spent here doing anything is guaranteed to be amazing. But I didn't want to blow all our money on accommodations and not have any money for trips out of the city. I randomly think of Fake Jacques and Quasi-Selena again. They've probably arrived at their destination by now, maybe a relative's house or a beautiful hotel. They've probably had a nice shower and are now settling in for a nap to combat the jet lag that's making my body feel like a sack of rocks. They'll no doubt have the money to hop up to Amsterdam or jaunt down to Italy, no problem. They looked sleek and cosmopolitan, like they'd reek of money and infinite possibilities. Hell, even the real Jacques and Selena are like that. Jacques parents sent him across the world for a whole year, and Selena's tans from her tropical family "vacays" barely have time to fade before she renews them in Hawaii or Belize. They don't have to worry about anything, while I've got to stretch my pennies that I earned at Safeway. Why is life so goddamn unfair?

I bite my lip and force myself to believe that this is okay. It *is* okay. It's *Paris*. Just being here is enough to make me feel lit up inside, and that would be the same even if I had to sleep under the *Pont Alexandre*. We'll do what Levi wants. Avoiding temper tantrums and freak-outs is of the utmost importance.

"Okay," I say shakily, letting out a long-held breath. "Okay, you're right."

We just stand there for a few minutes. I hear snatches of French, English, German, and Japanese all around us. A couple on a Vespa whips by, the girl squealing and clutching at her skirt as it blows up past her knees. A cloud obscures the sun for a few minutes and sinks us into a cool shadow. The cloud breaks apart and twin rays of light fall directly on the towers of Notre Dame and it takes my breath away.

"So? What should we do?" Levi asks.

"Find a hotel, I guess. And then enjoy our first day here."

*Find a hotel*—three words describing an action that should be fairly simple, especially in a touristy city like Paris. And it's true, physically locating hotels is easy. But finding ones with last-minute vacancies in the dying days of summer? Another story.

At first we stick to the immediate area, wandering around, inquiring at all the hotels we see. It soon becomes apparent that nobody within sight of the Seine has any rooms free, or at least not for less than a fortune per night. The weight of our jetlag begins to drag me down. Every flower bed we pass looks like a tempting place to nap. Levi wants to keep wandering, but I force us to do something reasonable: find a visitor's information center of some sort. I'm so tired, the sidewalk looks as comfortable as a memory foam mattress.

There, we get directions to a little hotel in the 13e *arrondissement*—far from the city center—called Hoteltastique. It's a measurement of how tired I am that the silly name on an outdated awning doesn't even bother me. The décor is very 1970s, but more grungy than retro cool. The elevator is rickety and the warped key barely fits into the warped lock on our warped door. I give Levi a look that says *I told you so*, but he doesn't notice.

Without even looking around the room, I collapse on one of the single beds and I'm instantly asleep.

# CHAPTER NINE

I wake up feeling not-quite-there. I'm in a room filled with bizarre orange light, surrounded by striped wallpaper, on a crisp, overly starched bedspread. The TV is on, spilling French words.

I remember where I am.

I sit up too fast. Blood rushes to my head.

Levi sits on the other bed, big hairy legs stretched out, staring at the TV. *American Idol* is on. Wait. I guess *French Idol*? The gaudy show logo spins across the screen. *Le Big Star!*

"What time is it?" I croak, rubbing the sleep from my eyes. I have that bizarre feeling of not knowing whether I should get up and have breakfast or sit down to eat dinner.

"Seven," Levi says. "Seven p.m."

I yawn, stretch my legs. Hunger stabs at my stomach.

"I'm starving," I say.

"Me too. You slept for forever."

"You could've woken me up."

He shrugs.

I pad into the bathroom and stare into my puffy face in the mirror. I cup my hands and take a gulp from the tap. The water tastes strange, kind of earthy. The edges of the tiles in the bathroom are worn and chipped, and the threshold between the room and the bathroom is slightly raised. I almost stubbed my toe. The room's carpet is flattened and worn, and God, could the sun be any freaking brighter?

I walk over to close the blinds when something catches my eye. The window opens onto the tiniest balcony I've ever seen, barely six inches of concrete surface between the window sill and a railing with cast-iron curls and ornate designs. I open the window. The sunshine is warm but tempered by a perfect breeze.

My feet and legs just barely fit on the balcony as I perch on the sill. We're on the second floor, maybe fifteen feet from the narrow street below. A group of middle-aged ladies enter the hotel below me, giggling. They must've had a lot of champagne at dinner. Motorcycles and scooters crowd the parking spaces. Across the street, the buildings know no logic. There's a small garage next to an even smaller shed next to an apartment building, and behind them are a cluster of tiny houses, and behind *them* are a few rows of apartment buildings. Alleys and tiny paths wind between all the buildings, but mostly I see rooftops. Some shorter, some a bit higher, but all so close together you could jump from roof to roof. Each rooftop has a different building material—terra cotta tiles, tin sheets, wood shingles—creating a mosaic of texture. The sunlight bathes it all.

"Hey, Levi," I call back into the room, where a cheesy French jingle plays. "We have a pretty neat view."

He shuffles over and stands behind me. "Huh."

"Sit down."

"Not enough room."

I scoot over.

Levi lowers himself to the ground very, very slowly. He sticks his feet out the window and crawls, crab-like, onto the sill. He takes up so much space he crushes me into the frame painfully. His feet are too big to rest on the tiny balcony, so he pokes them through the railing. When did they grow so huge? I stretch my memory back and remember his soft, little feet paddling in swimming pools with me, kicking at my sides in play fights. Now they're almost twice as big as mine, calloused and hairy like a hobbit's.

He glances down the street, both ways, like he's about to cross it. "I've never stayed in a hotel with a balcony before. It's nice."

"Yes, you have, when we went down to Portland to visit Josh's parents for Christmas. That hotel had a balcony overlooking the pool, remember?"

He blinks. "I didn't go to Portland."

"Yes, you did, we all did."

"No, Keira, you idiot," he snaps. "I stayed behind and Grandma watched me. God, you have the worst memory ever."

Oh my God, he's right. It was maybe two years ago, and the first time we'd spent Christmas anywhere but home. Josh pleaded with Levi to come with the rest of us, but Levi refused. He stayed home, with Grandma popping in to check on him when she could. He was supposed to go our grandparents' house for Christmas Day, but when we returned the next day, we found him playing Xbox in the basement with a giant bowl of cheeseballs. Orange crumbs were everywhere, caked over the front of Levi's T-shirt. Grandma told Mom that Levi had refused to go to her house, refused to eat Christmas dinner with her and Grandpa, so she'd given in after hours of trying to persuade him.

He had spent that Christmas alone.

"Hey . . . what did you do that Christmas, while we were gone?" I ask him now.

He shrugs. "Watched home movies."

I can almost see him in the winter-dark basement, messy hair silhouetted against the TV as it shows him grainy footage of us. It's the loneliest thing I could imagine.

"Really?"

"Yeah. There were a lot of horrible ones of you, singing the songs from that stupid boyband you loved."

"To the Starz?" I laugh. "Remember how you used to insert 'poo' and 'bum' into the lyrics?"

Levi laughs. Actually laughs.

"'Ooh, girl, I love your blue BUM and long blond POO,'" he sings.

I launch into Levi's classic rendition of their other hit, "Complicated." "'When you're with me, I never feel CONSTIPATED.'"

We both dissolve into laughter.

"You used to annoy me so much," I say, wiping away an errant tear. Where'd that come from? "But I guess you were pretty funny."

"Hindsight is twenty-twenty," Levi says. "Now you recognize my poetic genius."

The sun starts to slip behind the rooftops. Night in Paris is about to begin, and I'm wide awake.

"Well?" I ask. "Should we go get some dinner?"

"Yes," he says right away. "I'm starving."

French food, here we come.

I figure the best way to locate a great restaurant is just to wander around until we find one. In minutes, we stumble upon a crêpe place. The name of the place—*Crêpes Pour Vous*—is so perfect.

"Yes. Crêpes for us. Thank you," I say to the sign above us as I open the door.

It's a tiny little place, with only a few tables crowded into a room smaller than my bedroom at home. The walls are covered in posters without a theme. Posters of food alongside posters of Jim Morrison, alongside a framed poster of the cast of *Friends* circa 1994, bad hair and all, grinning down at us.

Before I can look at the menu, my eyes lock onto the boy behind the counter. He fiddles with a radio, frowning as he turns a stiff, ancient dial. He has deep brown hair that falls into his eyes and cheekbones sharp enough to cast shadows down his face. I can only see him from the chest up over the high counter, but it's enough to know he's totally hot.

Hot Crêpe looks up. His gaze spears me, taking in my tangled, curly brown hair and freckled, heart-shaped face. I start to feel tingling along the parts of my body I wish were smaller—my thighs, my stomach, my flabby upper arms. I suck in and draw my shoulders back.

Oh God. I have to order food from him, while being completely starving but not wanting to look like a huge fatso who routinely shoves twenty whole crêpes into her mouth. But it's either that or go hungry. I hate girls who are afraid to eat in front of boys.

I was that girl around Jacques. Screw it. I'll eat what I want.

Hot Crêpe raises an eyebrow. That's as close as he comes to "Hi, welcome to *Crêpes Pour Vous*, how may I help you?"

"Hi, um . . . *bonne soir*." I smile. My cheeks are on fire. I glance at the menu and realize I have no idea what I want to eat. "Um . . ."

Hot Crêpe turns back to the radio, dialing past some droning French talk show.

"Take your time," he mutters in a thick accent.

It looks like I'm going to have to, because there are so. Many. Choices. Dessert crêpes, slathered in whipped cream and strawberries and chocolate and, God help me, Nutella. Savory crêpes, with all manner of meat and cheese, egg, and delectable-looking sauces. What's a girl to do? Hot Crêpe's lip curls in frustration as the radio imports only static. I'd hate to have that scowl turned on me.

"What do you think?" I ask Levi.

"I just want a plain one," he says. "No, four plain ones."

"Plain? No topping or anything?"

He nods.

*Hi, handsome crêpe maker, I'd like four crêpes. Nope, nothing on them. Just four plain-ass pancakes for my weirdo brother.*

This is always the way with Levi, every time we go out to a restaurant. He's too shy to talk to waiters, so Mom or I have to explain exactly how plain he wants his food—which is *very* plain, but with an inexplicable amount of pickles. There's always an embarrassing ordeal if an order comes out wrong. Levi will huff and puff, moan loudly, and as recent as two years ago, he would even cry or collapse on the ground. What if that happens here? He's already curling his lips, looking at the dirty linoleum floor. I don't know if my fledgling French can properly explain Levi.

I take a deep breath. What Levi wants, Levi has to get, or I'll never hear the end of it. And there's no Mom here to handle a tantrum. I step up to the counter. The boy is washing his hands at a tiny sink.

"*Bonjour,*" I say. "May I please . . . um, *avoir quatre crêpes,* plain? *Avec . . . avec rien . . .*"

He glances up from the towel he wipes his hands with. One eyebrow raises almost imperceptibly. "Speak English. It will be easier on everyone."

*Uh.* "But I need to practice my French."

He lifts a corner of his mouth. I guess that passes for a smile.

"Practice on someone else."

My skin tingles. He keeps drying his hands like this—this *insult*—is nothing to him.

"I want four totally plain crêpes, all on one plate, and then one Nutella crêpe. *Please.*" Screw dinner. I'll skip right to dessert. *Vive la France.*

The jerk just shrugs.

I shake—in anger or anticipation—as Crêpe Jerk performs his art. He pours batter onto the hot plate, then swirls a little wooden tool in a circle to spread the batter paper-thin. He uses a metal spatula to flip the crêpe in one quick motion, making it look effortless.

He makes Levi's, folding and stacking them concentrically on a plate, then he makes mine, slathering it with Nutella. I have to actively stop myself from slobbering. He hands me the plates and his dark eyes gaze at me across the sugar-dusted chocolate. Despite his new nickname, Crêpe Jerk, I swoon a little bit.

I pay, grab plastic knives and forks, and sit down with Levi. Crêpe Jerk goes back to fixing his radio, scowl in place.

As angry as he made me, *commanding* me to speak English, I can't help but wonder what it would be like to fall head-over-heels in love with him. If this was a movie, that would have been our disastrous first meeting with awful first impressions. It's classic, circa *Pride and Prejudice*. I'll keep coming back to this restaurant, and we'll have witty repartee and pretend to hate each other. Then we'll share a few tender, illuminating moments, and then it'll be time for me to leave Paris. Somehow I won't be able to get in contact with him to tell him I'm going, so I'll leave him a letter telling him how I've always loved him since the first time I met him. In French—and my written French is much better than my spoken French. He'll be so moved and overwhelmed by his love for me that he'll follow me to the airport to pledge his everlasting love. Then I'll move to Paris to be with him. Happily ever after. Cue end credits.

I catch myself smiling at him and I have to remind myself that none of that has happened yet.

He looks up and sees me staring. I drop my gaze to my crêpe, cut a dainty piece, and eat it like a lady. I look back up. His lips twist in a smile, like Levi's sometimes do, but this isn't a smile trying to hide gleeful laughter. This is a cruel, mocking smile, exactly like Jacques's.

Another cook comes out of the back room. He speaks a flood of rapid French, something about something that's lost, with some curse words thrown in. Crêpe Jerk replies, then whispers something. His eyes slide over to me. Cook #2 looks at me too, wearing the same smirk.

They laugh. I hear them drawl a couple of words in a way exaggerated American accent. *Bun-joor.*

"*Quatre crêpes avec rien,*" the hot one says, over-pronouncing every word, using a q-sound and pronouncing the s's, which I *didn't even do.*

I look down at my plate. I should hurl it at them right now, splatter the Nutella all over their stupid grins.

"Do you like your crêpes?" I ask Levi, just to keep my mind off *them.*

"Mhmm." His mouth makes smacking noises. He's never been able to control his gross eating sounds. "They might be better if they were thicker."

"Then they'd be pancakes."

"Maybe I just like pancakes better."

Oh God, I hope the French idiots didn't hear that. Just what I need, more fuel for their fire. American kids who complain that crêpes aren't like Betty Crocker pancakes.

As I watch, Levi lifts his crêpes to his mouth with his hands. His knife and fork lie abandoned on the tabletop.

"Levi, use your cutlery!"

Words Mom has cried a bazillion times. I recognize that, but it doesn't stop me from lunging forward and shoving his knife and fork toward him.

He glares. "Why? Mom isn't here."

"There's such a thing as table manners here." *Please don't give them another reason to laugh at us*, I add silently.

He fumbles his fork and almost drops it. I reach over and cut his crêpes into pieces for him. Just like Mom does, like he's a perpetual child, never going to grow into a functional adult.

"There," I say. I let my knife clatter against my plate when I'm done. "*Now* eat them."

He holds his fork in his fist and stabs the crêpe pieces, shoving them in his mouth and only swallowing when he can't close his mouth anymore.

The Crêpe Losers are laughing even harder. I have maybe a bite and a half left, and a smear of Nutella on the paper plate. I feel apathetic toward it.

"Come on, Levi," I say, standing up. "Let's go."

My brother grabs the last few bites of his crêpes—in his hands—and follows me out the door. The losers don't see fit to lower their voices anymore. Before we've gone completely, I catch the words "*la p'tite dame et le gros.*" Accompanied by more laughter, of course.

The little lady and the fat one. *Le gros.* One adjective to encompass a whole person.

The French language can be so cruel.

I always hoped—naively, I guess—that the French were above making fun of someone for something as stupid as their size. I hoped Jacques would be one crappy exception to a rule of French magnanimity. I always thought they'd pick on table manners or fashion sense before they stooped as low as weight. Levi has three strikes there. No table manners to speak of, tear-away athletic pants and oversize hoodie, and he's awfully large.

I hate myself for caring what those guys think. I hate myself for wanting Levi to conform so I look better in front of—ugh—cute guys. I've made sacrifices for guys so many times, and for what? So I could be uncomfortable but deemed worthy in the eyes of losers who make fun of strangers?

I'm horrible.

We wander after we leave *Crêpes Pour Vous*. The street is lined with restaurants, and I can see the glowing, happy diners through the windows. I feel like I need to move, run wild, shake off the dust of who I've always been. Wipe the crêpe shop jerks from my mind.

"So?" Levi mumbles. His crêpes are gone, a couple crumbs clinging to his lips. "What do we do now?"

The sun has only just set. The lights of Paris come alive around us. A slight breeze raises the hairs on my arms. It's our first night in Paris. We should find an adventure.

That's when I see it: a poster in a bus shelter, with the words *Louvre La Nuit!* Remove the L and it sounds like *ouvre la nuit*, "open the night." Words that are now stuck in my head.

"Levi," I say, pointing to it. "There. That's where we're going. The Louvre."

# Chapter Ten

The metro stop is called, very appropriately, *Palais Royal Musée du Louvre*. The station empties directly into the underground lobby of the Louvre. My low mood from earlier has reversed. Now I'm giddy.

"Holy shit," I say, laughing. "Levi, this is it. This is the *Louvre*."

"Yeah, duh," he murmurs. His eyes travel up the famous inverted pyramid that dominates the lobby to the night sky overhead.

The room is rosy and dark like a fancy cocktail reception. People crowd around, taking pictures and posing. A man holds a giant iPad aloft, filming the whole lobby. Two girls, faces pressed together, hold a phone at arm's length. They tilt their heads this way and that, staring at the screen, puckering their lips *just right*. It takes them a good minute before they actually take the photo, and then they examine it, delete it, and retake it.

I reach for my camera and realize I left it on the desk in the hotel room. I only have my cell phone. I take that out and—

Levi rolls his eyes violently. "Ughhh, don't take pictures with that thing. If you turn into one of these fucking losers, I won't talk to you all fucking trip."

"It's the Louvre, Levi. I'm going to want memories."

"So *remember it*. We have these things called brains, Keira, that can remember things. You should try using yours."

My phone sits, enormous, in my little pale hand. I'm not a phone addict by any means, but I take pictures of things that are important. This? The Louvre? *Important!* And he's going throw a fit about it? To get through this with no tears, no stomping feet, no shouting, I'm going to end up sitting in my bedroom some-day thinking, "I once went to the Louvre" and having nothing to prove that fact to myself. Memories will fade and someday this night will feel like a dream.

It's that and make Levi happy, or trade my brother for photographs.

I shove my phone to the very bottom of my bag and we get in line to buy tickets. He's right: if I see the Louvre entirely through my cell phone's camera lens instead of with my own eyes, I'll regret it.

Whether it's artistic and architectural beauty overload or the jetlag, the Louvre already feels like a dream and I'm walking through fog. Some people meander about the corridors, some stride forward purposefully. According to the museum map that somehow ended up in my hands, there are approximately one million wings and exhibits we could go to, and they all sound fascinating: Greek, Etruscan, and Roman Antiquities. Egyptian Antiquities. Near Eastern Antiquities. A section dedicated to the history of the Louvre itself, where you can descend into the earth to see what remains of the old palace's moat. The Denon wing, full of Caravaggios and Rembrandts and one very special da Vinci.

That perks me up. I poke Levi and point to one of the signs with Mona Lisa's silhouette, showing the way to *La Joconde,* as she's called in French. "Shall we go find her?"

He shrugs. I take that as a yes.

The Louvre has long fascinated me—I know, me and the rest of humanity—but I've always refrained from buying one of those massive books with pictures of the entire collection. I wanted to be surprised when I finally got here. When we enter a cavernous hall via an infinite staircase, stone arching impossibly high overhead, it's all made worth it.

A storm-gray statue holds court at the top of the stairs. An angel, judging by her wings, although she's missing her head and arms. Her chest is thrust forward, her dress billowing behind her in the wind. I have to convince myself that she's carved in stone and real wind isn't flowing through fabric. She's dazzling.

The crowd parts around her, and people flow to the left or right, pausing to look but mostly passing by. I step forward—I have to at least find out her name.

WINGED VICTORY, the sign says. THE GODDESS NIKE. FOUND ON THE GREEK ISLAND OF SAMOTHRACE.

"Like the running shoes," Levi says in his signature monotone. I roll my eyes.

There's a glass case near the sign, holding a beat-up hand and a few crumbled pieces of stone.

"It's supposed to be her right hand," Levi says, reading the plaque. "And some of her other fingertips. How the hell do they know that? She doesn't have arms!"

"*Found on the same site eighty-seven years later,*" I read.

"That doesn't mean anything."

"Found on the same site, fits in place . . ."

"How would it fit in place?" he says. "*She doesn't have arms!*"

"Levi, it's simple science. They could obviously carbon date the stone and find out it's a match."

"Do you even know what carbon dating is?" Levi asks.

I don't. But he doesn't have to know that.

"Levi, it's the Louvre," I say. "They wouldn't exhibit anything if they weren't completely sure it was authentic."

"How do you know?"

"*Because it's the Louvre*. It's only the most famous museum on the planet!"

"Yeah, which means they could display tons of fraudulent artifacts and no one would question them," he says. "Everyone would just swallow the Kool-Aid like good little art-worshipers. Idiots."

I wonder if he realizes that it hurts me when he insults groups of people that include me. It was easy to shake off when we were young and he was being the typical little brother, hating everything I liked. Now that we're almost adults, sometimes it feels like it might be real.

I grab his sleeve and steer him away.

The rest of the Louvre is nothing like that vast hall, all stone, showcasing one spectacular piece of art. Now we're in a world of gilded moldings and frescoes by geniuses. Paintings litter the walls. We continue on a fast track to the Mona Lisa's room because any time I stop to look at something for more than a second, Levi growls deep in his throat like an animal. It hurts my heart, having to stride past paintings and statues I want to lose myself in.

Now I understand how Mom feels, having to bypass beautiful things. This is Mom's book club, trips to the gym, her time playing *Stones of Zendar*. These are the things she covets in antique stores or even just the clothing section at Target, where she routinely buys new blouses and returns them the next day to use the money for other things—like Levi's medical bills, now. She must feel like her whole life is one big sacrifice.

I bypass a wall-sized Caravaggio and my heart wants to break out of my chest and leap toward it.

There's a huge bottleneck in the doorway to the Mona Lisa's room.

"What do you like about the Mona Lisa?" I ask Levi as the human traffic blocks us.

Levi shrugs. "I guess it's that Leonardo da Vinci painted it. He's probably the biggest genius who ever lived."

"Yeah," I agree. "But the painting itself?"

"I dunno. It looks nice. And it's just really famous and stuff." He frowns down at me out of the corner of his eye. "What else do you want me to say?"

"What else do you want to say?"

"Nothing." He stands up on his tiptoes. "Oh my God, did everyone just forget how to walk?"

"Shh!" I hiss.

"I want them to hear me, then they might *move* . . ."

My brother, giving everybody one more reason to hate American tourists. I wince an apology at a slick, suited man who shoots him a look. I wish I could tell everyone "he has autism or something," but I don't want to write him off with one word, like he isn't a full person. I don't want to be Dr. Pearson.

It takes twenty minutes to get close enough to see the painting. Levi groans and growls and stamps his feet the whole time. "God, can't we just go?" he complains.

"Don't you want to see it?"

"Not this much!" Someone brushes past him and Levi glares after them. "Ugh, it smells in here. Like rusty nails and farts."

I snort. He frowns deeper.

"Hang on just a bit longer, okay? We're almost there."

And then I catch a glimpse of the Mona Lisa through the crowd, still twenty feet away, and I understand the reason for the traffic jam. Her knowing smile stops you in your tracks. *Beautiful* isn't the word. It's more like . . .

"*Elle m'arrête*," a French woman says to her companion, laughing.

*She stops me.* She arrests me. Yeah. *Arresting* is the word. I imagine all the history that must have passed her painted eyes. She stared for years into the eyes of da Vinci, then for centuries into the eyes of her royal buyers and countless caretakers. Then the eyes of thieves, then, finally, people who came from around the world just to see her. Millions of eyes, it must be. Maybe even billions.

What effect will those painted eyes have on Levi? If he feels any of the awe I feel . . . I imagine the frown lines melting away. Those brown eyes losing their anger and frustration. His face taking on an air of peace, for once.

"Can you see her?" I whisper to Levi.

I look up at him. He peers over the tops of peoples' heads with a disinterested grimace. "It's exactly how it looks in pictures."

Not at all. The colors are darker and more striking in person, the contrasts starker. If Levi doesn't see that, then she definitely hasn't affected him or brought him any kind of peace.

"Let's go," Levi says, tugging hard on my sleeve. "*Now.*"

His hand squeezes just above my elbow, too tight, too tight. As he drags me away, I turn and catch one last glimpse of the painting as she slips out of my view. If I'd had my way, I'd have stood there for hours, holding her gaze. But no—it's always Levi who gets what he wants. He always got to pick when we left the playground, when we were done sledding or skating or swimming. His patience would snap and Mom would collect all our things and whisk us away, always ages before I was done. I was always the one who had to suffer at those times. Mom always cut Levi's suffering short. It was always me, watching the fun through the rear window, lower lip stuck out and quivering.

He drags me back out to the main gallery, which is far less crowded. Apparently, everyone in the entire museum has flocked to the Mona Lisa at this precise moment. Levi slows once we're out here. He still has his so-pissed-off-it's-unreal face on, but now that the crowds are gone, I think he's better.

"So?" I say with a sigh. "What should we see next?"

Levi's face softens after a few minutes, his clenched jaw loosening.

"The Egyptian stuff," he says. "That oughtta be good, since France has such a boner for Egypt."

I snort in laughter. "It totally does."

The Egyptian Antiquities department occupies a few floors, one of them below ground. The rooms are still big and airy, though; light stone walls kept bright. It's almost empty, just a few other visitors. An enormous sphinx dominates the first room.

"Egyptian faces are always smiling," I say.

"That's racist," Levi monotones.

I laugh. "I mean, their art. Sphinxes and masks and gods. They always have this . . . smirk, y'know?"

"They're creepy as fuck," he says.

The sphinx smiles, face pointed straight ahead as she crouches, waiting for . . . something.

"Yeah," I say. "They are."

Levi has wandered off, up some stairs, into the rest of the Egyptian Antiquities section. I follow him, looking over my shoulder. The Sphinx still smiles straight ahead. Still waits.

Glass cases surround us on all sides in the next room, holding ancient textiles and pottery. Tall, skinny vases etched with stripes catch my eye. The plaque tells me they're a thousand years older than Jesus. Levi is across the room, staring into another glass case. He doesn't answer when I tell him about the pre-Jesus pots. He keeps staring.

It's a mummy. On its back, its arms crossed over its chest. A shiver slips down my spine. I've always *hated* mummies. Loved Ancient Egypt, hated mummies. Ever since a sixth-grade field trip to a museum where my friend Katie dared me to stare at the most gruesome, badly-preserved mummy Egypt could have produced for a whole minute. My stupid, overactive imagination burned the dried skin and gouged-out eye sockets into my nightmares for years. That mummy was just a kid. I was scared, but also really sad for him.

This mummy is different. It's impeccably preserved; its wrappings look like they could have been done yesterday. If you were to unwrap the fingers, they'd be supple and flexible, with an iron grip. Biceps are still defined, hamstrings and calf muscles still evident. Take away the glass case and this could be a person in a costume, waiting to jump up and scare us.

Except for the head, wrapped so tightly the skull looks small and painfully vulnerable. The only traces of features are slightly crumbling lumps where ears should be. Its face is concealed by a mesmerizing pattern of square, concentric folds. If there was a face, the outer squares would frame it, but the frame just frames more of itself. Does the mummy have a face? What would it look like, if I undid each pristine fold? I don't want to know.

I rub my arms to ward away the goose bumps but skin on skin can't cure my fear. I have become one big goose bump, one big shudder. The place is full of mummies, I realize then. Millions of them, standing around, waiting for *something*. So many bodies, their faces staring at me.

"Oh God, why are there so many?" I murmur to Levi.

"So many what?"

"Mummies."

"There's only one, Keira."

"What about all these?" I point around at all the bemused Egyptian faces, cat's eye makeup and mischievous eyes. Sarcophagi. Even the word is terrifying. And there are so many. Around every corner, another vessel meant to hold dead bodies. They may not have bodies inside them, but I can't convince myself I'm not entirely surrounded by death—it's in the walls, under the floor. I swear there are ghosts walking among us. I turn around, but having the mummy at my back only raises more chills. Across the room, a giant Anubis's pointed, grotesquely sly face leers. He holds a staff, points it at me, like he's casting a spell that's making me feel tight, small, like my lungs are canisters that don't contain the air they should. The walls close in. My head feels strained and tired and liable to collapse.

I have to get out of here.

"Keira, where are you going? Hey!"

I'm in a different room. I've turned too many corners. Levi shuffles behind me, like I'm leading him somewhere useful. I enter another room through an arched doorway—I'm sure this is the room we first entered—but it's another wrong turn. Through the windows I can see the quadrangle outside and the lights of the Louvre against the black sky and oh my God, we can't get out. What if we're stuck? What if we die here?

Levi almost joined these bodies two months ago. Levi *wanted* to join these bodies.

I can't breathe. I'm on the floor now, in a corner, not sure how I got here.

"Keira?" Levi's voice is part of the fog. He's standing above me. I try to make words, but with no breath I just . . . just . . .

"Come on, Keira, God!"

Now tears blur my vision. The words won't come so the tears jump to replace them, like *that* will do a goddamn thing to help.

"*Mademoiselle? Monsieur?*" a man says. "*Est-elle OK?*"

Levi doesn't speak French; he can't answer. He's awkwardly silent, but his eyes are alive, alive and full of worry. The man who asked the question looks between the two of us, confused, backing away like he's going to leave us here.

"Help!" I gasp. "Exit, exit . . . *sortie?*"

He points. A red exit sign blinks just above us.

Levi moves in that direction, grabbing my arm to tug my frozen body off the floor.

Walking, letting Levi lead, I start to relax. Holy shit, what just happened to me? My whole body burns, hums, tingles. Shock numbs my fingertips and toes. What *was* that?

Why were the ancient Egyptians so obsessed with death? So obsessed with some afterlife, where they would supposedly need their withered-up bodies and jars of intestines. That's not what death is, passing through a veil and coming out the other side to party with the ancestors or whatever. Death is permanent. Death is absolute. Death is inescapable, even when you devote every moment to stopping it from entering your mind.

We don't say anything as we leave the Louvre, climbing the staircase that surfaces inside the above-ground glass pyramid. My weakness, my sudden inability to function—it all goes unspoken. I feel heavy, and I realize how jet-lagged I am, with too few hours of sleep. Not helping.

Once we're outside in the enormous courtyard with the wind whipping around us, my body loosens. I'm still vibrating, but I can breathe here. I can admire the Louvre's façade, lit up like it might have been in its past life as a royal palace. We sit down on a bench to admire the glass pyramid as it sparkles against the sky.

"Overrated," Levi says. "Waste of space."

I want to launch a counter-argument, but exhaustion has caught up with me and adrenaline and fear have worn me even thinner. And I secretly think he might be right.

We wander back to the metro and drag our tired bodies through the streets to Hoteltastique. It's only when we're stumbling back to our room that I realize Levi never let go of my arm.

# CHAPTER ELEVEN

Levi wakes up before me. He has the TV blasting. The room is full of ripe, late-morning sunlight. I feel like my body is less than substantial; someone could reach right through me. I'm so hungry I could eat the comforter off the bed, hotel germs included.

"I need to brush my teeth," I say, getting out of bed and heading straight for the bathroom. "And then we need to eat. Like, *yesterday.*"

I dig our toiletry bag out of my suitcase and head into our tiny bathroom. I set up my moisturizer and cleanser on the little shelf along with my toothbrush. Levi's toothbrush goes on the other side, far away from mine—if he uses the wrong one, he'll literally puke.

Levi has set out his medications. Three bottles and a little pill tray, the days of the week labeled, pills all ready to go. I recognize them all from Mom's flashcards but couldn't name them if you paid me. I check to make sure the right amount of each pill is in each slot and wonder if they are the only things keeping him here.

I shake myself. Can't let my mind go there. I can't get scared.

"We should go to McDonald's," Levi says in the next room.

"We'll find a café or something," I call back. "I didn't come all this way for McDonald's."

"I don't want Frenchy-French food," Levi murmurs. "I just want hashbrowns."

"Come on, Levi," I sigh. "We're going to have a real French breakfast and that's that."

I shower. Levi doesn't. He's starting to smell, but I don't want to provoke him any more than I already have. Because he's crying as we leave the hotel.

Not crying, exactly. Death-glaring and surreptitiously wiping his eyes. I don't care; I'm not giving him what he wants this time. I want to cram myself full of something heavy and gourmet—sausage, eggs, bacon, that kind of breakfast.

I'm so hungry I can't really concentrate on finding that, though. All the bistros in our neighborhood are either still closed or serving lunch food. I stalk the streets like a zombie hunting for brains. Or Eggs Benedict.

Just kitty-corner from our hotel, we pass an open doorway and I smell it: baking bread.

I barrel inside, attracted like the north to the south pole of a magnet.

The bakery's glass case is chock full of heaven. Marzipan blobs, sugared and shaped like animals. Cookies of every shape and size, filled with jam, shaped like flowers, dipped in dark chocolate. Huge discs of puff pastry, encrusted with cinnamon and sugar and shaved almonds and a million other delicious things. Bouquets of baguettes, some still steaming, filling the air with the sweet, enveloping scent of bread. And, of course, the croissants: shining with butter, piled on top of each other like they're just clambering to be chosen. The young woman behind the counter smiles indulgently at us. Her cheeks are as round and red as literal apples, punctuated by dimples on either side of her mouth. She raises her eyebrows in a question.

"*Deux croissants, s'il vous plaît,*" I blurt out to her. "*Deux croissants* and . . . and . . . a baguette, and one of those cookies with the jam, and one of those chocolate-dipped ones, and one of those big round things."

Her eyes widen and she waves her hands. "*Je m'excuse,*" she says. "My English is not the best."

Whoops. And here I am, spewing English all over her counter.

"*Pardonnez-moi!*" I say, trying to make it sound like I'm pouring my heart and soul into the words. I know how it feels to have a language you're just learning come flying at you.

She smiles, blushing. "*Qu'est-ce que vous vouliez?*"

*What would I like?* I point and try my hardest to read out the names on the placards in perfect French. *Baguette* is easy. *Croissant* is a little strenuous on my accent. *Pain aux raisins*, the big flat disc coated with glaze and raisins, is freaking hard.

She wraps the baguette in paper and puts each item onto a beautiful china plate, not into a flimsy paper bag like Starbucks. Paris has one-upped you again, Seattle. She arranges the items on a big wooden tray, and while she does it, she looks up at me and smiles, her eyes crinkling. I can just feel joy pouring out of her. Definitely beats the bored baristas.

I take out a handful of Euros but she waves her hand.

"After, pay," she says. "First, enjoy."

We sit down at a table built into the shop's bay window. The old glass warps the Parisians walking by. A couple people glance toward the open door of the bakery, but no one comes in.

When I take the first bite of a croissant, my heart despairs for all the billions of people on earth who are not eating this particular croissant *right now.* It's more than flaky and buttery; it's silk made of dreams, melting against my tongue.

I devour the first in mere seconds and reach for another. Tears spring to my eyes and I laugh, spluttering pastry flakes everywhere, when I discover the chocolate at its center. Chocolate! In a croissant! What could be more marvelous?

Levi shoots me a *have you lost your mind?* kind of look, which just makes me laugh harder.

"Izzogud!" I blurt out around my mouthful of deliciousness.

Levi's eyes crinkle into slits as he chews. His shoulders spasm. He's laughing.

I can't stop laughing, either. I move on to one of the jam-filled shortbread cookies, which is covered in a glaze so smooth and soft it makes an audible *pfff* sound against my teeth. Next I tear into a baguette, which you'd think would be boring because it's just plain bread, but it's the sweetest, fluffiest bread. Like marshmallows in bread form.

Of course, one cannot simply eat this much pastry without almost becoming sick. By the time we've cleared all our plates, both Levi and I are groaning as we collect every last crumb with our fingers.

"That was *amazing*," I splutter, leaning back in my chair, thankful for yoga pants. "Sheer, unadulterated amazingness. Wasn't it amazing?"

"Yeah," he admits. "Better than anything you ever made."

I blush. Last year, I went through a baking phase where I tried out complicated French recipes I had no business attempting. Let's just say it was a miserable failure. Levi complained for a week about the lingering stench of my very-*brûlée crème brûlée*.

I go back to the counter to pay the woman for our garden of earthly delights. While she's counting back my change, I want to tell her to keep the change as a tip. Is tipping encouraged or frowned upon in France? I guess I didn't memorize that part of the travel books.

I fumble out the words "do you want to keep the change?" in French. Her mouth pops open. Her already rosy cheeks flush even harder.

"*Ahh, non!*" she blurts out. "*Non, non, je ne peux pas.*" She presses the coins into my hands and holds hers up afterward, waving them profusely.

"*Pardon,*" I murmur, lowering my head. "I—I didn't mean to . . ."

"*Non, non,*" she says again. "I mean simply . . . you must keep your money."

I smile. "Thank you so much. Everything was delicious."

Her eyes crinkle again. "*Merci à vous.*"

We stagger back onto the street, narrowly missing a fancy-looking business man, young and bald, who glances into the *pâtisserie* but walks on.

All of Paris lies before us now.

"Well?" I ask Levi. "What should we do today?"

I can't tell if he's scowling or just squinting in the sun.

"I don't know," he says. "Something."

"Should we go somewhere awesome?" I reach into my travel purse for some of the brochures we picked up at the airport.

A lot of them are brochures for museums. Musée D'Orsay, le Centre Pompidou, Museum of This, Museum of That . . . I flip past those. *So* not in the mood for museums after last night. That leaves us with tours. The Loire Valley. A day trip down south, to the glass-blue Mediterranean Sea. A day trip to Holland. A day trip that takes you through Flanders Fields and to all the war memorials and famous sites of battles. This interests Levi.

"It'd be cool to see trenches," he says.

Maybe that would draw Levi out of his shell a bit. I imagine him maybe meeting some veterans, men who were there for all the historical events he watches documentaries about. Maybe he'd ask them questions and care about their answers. I'd be able to text Mom something happy.

And then I remember all the blurry black-and-white photos they showed in history class. Blown-apart bodies camouflaged with mud and the hollow, empty gazes of soldiers. I shiver. Trenches would get under my skin even worse than mummies.

"I don't think so," I say.

"That's like, the *one* thing I wanted to do here."

"What about Versailles, or the Eiffel Tower?"

"I want to see war stuff." He sticks his hands in his hoodie pocket, glaring.

"Well . . . there is the war museum, *Les Invalides*."

He looks at me and raises an eyebrow. I take it as my cue to pull out my guidebook. I read off a couple of the exhibits, names of cannons and guns I couldn't care less about, until this: "The Tomb of Napoleon?" I blink to make sure I read that right. "Holy crap. Let's go see Napoleon's tomb!"

"Huh."

"Does that mean yes?"

He nods. "Let's go visit Napoleon Bonaparte. I'm sure he'll be very glad to see us."

"Welcoming and accommodating," I agree.

⸙⸙⸙

We emerge from the depths of the Invalides metro station into "oh my God"-worthy territory. The Seine is on our left, flowing lazily under the Pont Alexandre, the most glorious bridge in existence. It's a wide, low expanse of white stone, all celebratory white pillars and crests and stone garlands. The gold statues on either end pose on giant pedestals. They sparkle in the sudden flashes of tourists' cameras. Beyond the bridge is a huge avenue with pristine grass on either side, stretching toward the gold pantheon, the dome beneath which Napoleon rests.

And looming on the horizon is the Eiffel Tower, tantalizingly close.

I can't believe we're here. I can't believe *I* got us here.

I point at the pantheon. "That's where Napoleon's tomb is."

Levi grunts. "Not bad."

"I'd say he did pretty well for himself."

We cross a busy street with a gaggle of other tourists, and as we amble down the forever-boulevard, Levi talks. "Depends on your definition of 'pretty well.' Yeah, he has a nice place now that he's long dead, and he's considered one of the greatest military commanders of all time, but he was exiled to far-off islands twice in his lifetime. Also, the autopsy said stomach cancer killed him, but a lot of people think it was arsenic poisoning."

"Isn't that kind of a *thing*, though?" I ask. "Important people from the past dying under slightly suspicious circumstances and everyone being like, 'it was arsenic poisoning'?"

"Everyone loves a conspiracy." Levi squints up at the dome of the Pantheon. A reflected sunbeam lights up his cheek with a square of gold. "Keeps things interesting."

"Some people think Jane Austen died of arsenic poisoning."

He barks in laughter. "Who'd wanna poison Jane Austen? Yeah, she was a real threat. *Sure*."

"Well, she *was* the greatest novelist of her time."

"That's hardly a reason to poison someone. You only poison important people."

"And Jane Austen isn't important?" My blood is starting to boil because my brother insulted Jane Austen in front of the Pantheon. My life is weird.

"Not important enough to assassinate."

"Some people might have wanted to assassinate her. Other writers, maybe? To claim to have written her novels, which were published anonymously?"

He makes a disgusted face. "You *actually* believe Jane Austen was poisoned? God, I knew you were dumb."

"*Levi!*"

"Well, you're being stupid."

"I never said I believed it, but God, you don't have to be such an asshole."

Stupid tears burn my eyes. I try to tell myself he doesn't mean it, doesn't mean to hurt people when he says stuff like that, but I'm not convinced.

"Jane Austen is so overrated. If you like her books you must—"

"Why do you have to judge everyone else for liking things you don't?" I snap.

"I can't help it if her books are so bad," he sneers.

"Shut *up*, Levi. I can't take your negativity, so shut up for like *one* second."

This is the conversation we're having in front of the ticket agent's booth to enter the military museum. The ticket lady looks concerned, but hands us our tickets and *bienvenue*'s us in.

I swallow my anger so Levi can have his. As always.

The military museum is nothing like the Louvre. Everything here is wide open, white, and clean, and a lot of displays are outdoors, to my relief. Under the soaring dome of the Pantheon, staring at Napoleon's red clay tomb, I don't feel menaced by death. I feel detached, but not in a bad way. I feel calm and peaceful as we glide through the place.

Levi wanders the courtyard, looking at all the cannons on display.

"Do you know *Les Misérables*?" I call to him.

"Isn't that the movie where Russell Crowe's singing is awful?"

"Yeah. But do you know the story?"

He shakes his head.

"These guns remind me of when the revolutionaries are putting up the barricades to try to stop the army."

"It takes place during the revolution?"

I nod.

"Huh," he says. "I thought it was just some historical romance."

"It's mostly about the war." I get a sudden idea. "I wonder if we could go see it. I mean, this is Paris. I'm sure it's playing somewhere."

"The movie?"

"No, the musical."

Levi groans. "I don't want to see a play where people prance around singing."

"There are lots of guns and bloody wounds," I offer. "Lots of people die. Pretty much everyone dies."

He sucks in a huge amount of air.

I sweeten the deal. "We can have crêpes for dinner before we go."

He exhales like a popping balloon. "Okay, fine."

That night, after eating crêpes cooked by a courteous man who didn't make fun of us, we make our way to the theatre district. When the teller told me the price for last-minute tickets, my heart disregarded anatomical rules and slipped into my stomach. For the two of us to see this show, it costs more than a night at our hotel. It's a bunch of meals. It costs the same as a day trip to tour castles in the Loire Valley.

A tuxedoed man takes our tickets and we enter the theatre. Everyone is wearing fancy clothes. Not exactly black tie, but enough to make me extremely self-conscious in my floral blouse and cable-knit cardigan and jeans, and downright embarrassed by Levi's sweatpants and rain boots. I skip the merchandise table, skip the snack bar. I just want us to disappear into the dark theatre.

The usher glances at our tickets and points at the ceiling. "The balcony," he says. "Up, up!"

"Uh . . ."

He jabs a finger to the right. Down a hallway is a dark flight of stairs, only a handful of theatre-goers on their way up. We follow them to a deserted second floor, where another usher shows us to our seats.

We're so far from the stage that it looks like a little diorama project made by a fourth grader. A three-digit price tag—in Euros—for this. Feeling disappointed comes with a side dish of feeling ungrateful. It's still *Les Mis*. It's still going to be awesome, crappy seats or not.

Levi lowers himself into his seat, taking forever to get comfortable. He wiggles and jiggles and sighs, finally settling on the most embarrassing position possible: slumped down so far his head is the only part of his body even resting against the back of the chair, his arms folded on his substantial belly. A woman down the row from us raises her eyebrows.

"You aren't going to be able to see anything," I tell him.

"I don't care."

"Fine." I get out some brochures and look over them in the dim house lighting. "Be miserable."

"It's in the title of the play," Levi says.

I smirk. "Very clever."

It seems like we wait an eternity, and Levi announces this about twenty times, but when the lights go down and the stage explodes into life, nothing matters anymore. Not the bad seats. Not the lady down the row, tsk-ing at us. Definitely not my lingering irritation with Levi. All I care about is Jean Valjean and the music that soars up from the orchestra, rattling my seat and gripping me by the throat.

I'm no theatre geek. I don't know any musicals by heart and I don't squeal at the mere mention of Stephen Sondheim. I've only seen *Les Misérables* because of a Hugh Jackman fangirl phase. I have an ebook copy of the novel I downloaded only because I knew it had to do with Paris and Victor Hugo wrote it, but I've never even opened the file.

Despite all that, watching it live is amazing. When Fantine sings "I Dreamed a Dream," my whole body trembles and tears pour down my face. When Jean Valjean runs from the law, I squeeze my crossed fingers so hard they ache through intermission. It feels like my will for him to escape is the only thing keeping him safe. I hated Cosette and Marius and their angsty romance in the movie, but here they make my heart flutter. And Eponine . . . when she sings her unrequited love song, "On My Own," the way

I was around Jacques comes rushing back. The actress whispers "I love him" repeatedly, and it chills me. She sings the last line and my cheeks burn in the darkness, even though I'm the only one who knows that that pining, pathetic character was me.

The whole show is chilling and amazing, but it isn't just the story and music doing it to me.

There's one character, one actor on stage, who captivates me. Enjolras. He's the leader of the revolution, the bright-eyed roguish friend of Marius. The actor's fervor is contagious; he makes me want to leap out of my chair and into battle with a bayonet. His hair, strawberry blond and wavy, breaks out from under his hat, and his costume has a swashbuckling flair to it, lots of movement, the character's daring all demonstrated in fabric. He's rash, he's overly optimistic, he only sees the glory of battle and not the imminence of his own death.

He's *super* hot.

He dies in a hail of bullets. I have to whisper to myself, *it's fiction, it's fiction, it's fiction*, and breathe deeply to stop my chest from caving in.

The play goes on and of course it's marvelous, the best thing I've ever seen, but then I notice that Levi is sleeping, mouth wide open. I'd hear snoring if the French Revolution wasn't raging. How could he fall asleep through trumpets and sword fights? I'm wired, and he's dead to the world in a room full of noise. And I paid a lot of money for the seat he's slumped in.

The show ends, and I rise with the crowd to give a standing ovation. With everyone on their feet, I can't see the stage anymore, and this becomes a problem when the cast is bowing and grinning and I can't see Enjolras. I stand on tiptoes, but no dice. I clap and clap and clap, and by the time I can see the stage again, the curtains are pulled and he's gone.

I wake Levi with a couple of shoves. He's instantly cranky.

"It's finally over?" he grumbles, stretching his arms above his head and almost hitting the old man trying to exit the row behind us.

I grab his wayward arm. "Careful! And yes, it's over. You slept through almost all of it."

"I saw enough to know that it was lame."

I feel like a punctured balloon. "Let's just go," I snap.

Of course, it isn't as easy as that. The theatre is so packed it takes ages to even get out onto the upper floor, never mind to descend the stairs to the lobby and leave. I have plenty of time to wallow in my misery, but I stave it off by flipping to the cast list in the big glossy show program.

It takes me a few minutes to find Enjolras, because actors always look ridiculously different in their professional head shots than on stage. His is combed and gelled like a 1940s rat-packer, with a crinkle-eyed smile. He looks much tamer than he did in character, but there's still something roguish in that smile. His name is Alec Rideout, and his bio says he's studied at Cambridge and Oxford. Wow.

I wonder what he's like in real life. If I were the kind of girl who did such things, I would want to search for him after the show and find out for myself.

My first instinct is to laugh at that thought. My second instinct is to do it.

I'm in France. If I don't take at least a few risks, do at least a few things that scare me, what use will any of this be? As we lumber slowly down the stairs to the lobby, I imagine it. Me, a naïve tourist. Him, a dashing British actor. I would coyly ask him for an autograph, and we would talk, and he would ask me out for a drink or something and we could spend an evening under the stars, gazing at the Eiffel Tower when it's all lit up and dazzling. My whole body tingles, imagining it.

"Levi," I say to the big lump shuffling along next to me. "I think I'm going to go find one of the actors."

He sighs the heaviest, world-weariest sigh I've ever heard. "That's *so* dumb."

"I don't care what you think. I'm going to do it."

"I'm not going with you."

"Just wait for me." We're in the lobby now. I scan around for a good meeting place. "How about that palm tree over there? Just go stand there. I'll probably be like, ten minutes."

Levi drags himself over to the palm tree, frown in place.

I have no idea how one would go about meeting an actor after a play, but taking a deep breath, I push against the flow of people exiting the theatre and find the nearest usher. I ask him if I can meet Alec Rideout.

The usher doesn't look at me. "Enter the stage," he says.

Enter the stage? I take that to mean the theatre. I push through the people and back into the emptying theatre. The curtain hides the stage, but as I watch, a girl's head pokes out and grins at the huge room. "Oh my God, this is what it's like being famous!" she says, in a broad Texas drawl. She withdraws but I hear her ask, "Can we go see your dressing room?"

In that moment, it's like the spirit of an adventurous girl possesses my body. I climb the stairs onto the stage and slip behind the heavy velvet curtain, into a world of darkness. I almost crash into a body lurking nearby. They don't seem to notice me. I stumble toward the light.

Dozens of people bustle around. The crew pushes set pieces back and forth, racks full of costumes rush by, and people yell a million directives into headsets. A few cast members are among the rushers. I start my stakeout.

There seem to be lots of hangers-on around, especially once I find the corridor full of dressing rooms. Names from the program adorn the doors, some open, some closed. I look for Alec Rideout and find his name listed on a shared dressing room. The door is open. I peek inside.

Three actors, in various stages of uncostuming themselves, laugh and shout together.

"I nearly tripped, rushing out from stage left," a British actor says. "Disguised it okay by pretending I just started jogging, but I'm sure Maurice caught it. Catches everything, he does."

"Nothing compares to my pants slipping down my ass during 'One Day More.' I thought for sure I was going to lose them." That voice sounds American.

"How were you, Alec?" the British one asks. My ears prick up. "How's your throat?"

"Bad," a voice says, weary and scratchy. "Very bad."

"That's not good," the American murmurs darkly. "You wouldn't want to let your understudy have a go."

"'S not that," he croaks.

"I'm just playing. But if you don't want my ugly mug taking center stage, you'll give your voice a rest, pronto."

Before I can come up with a plan, a tall, broad man in revolutionary garb, hair still stuck to his forehead with sweat from the night's performance, waltzes out the door and right into me.

"Whoa, there!" He grabs my arms to steady me, even though I don't really need steadying. "Who's this, then?"

"Um, I'm—I'm looking for Alec Rideout?"

"Alec! Someone here for you! Go on." He gives me a push into the room. "Just don't keep him talking all night. His voice is squeakin' like a prepubescent's."

And then I'm standing in the same room as the actors I watched all night on stage. One, the not–Alec Rideout, leans against the vanity counter and pulls off his eighteenth-century puffy shirt. He puts on a plain T-shirt and rather pointedly leaves the room.

Alec Rideout himself sits at the vanity, head in his hands, shoulders bent forward. Beside him, a kettle bubbles away, steaming up the mirror. He looks miserable as he glances up at my reflection in the mirror.

"Can I help you?"

His voice is so pained, I wince and reach for my own throat. "Oh, um, I don't want to trouble you," I stutter. "If you want, I can just go."

He sighs and shakes his head.

"I just wanted an autograph." My program slips between my sweaty palms. "I thought you were amazing tonight."

He smiles faintly and reaches out his hand. I give him my program.

"What did you like in particular?" he asks in that faint voice.

"Your . . . passion." The word almost makes me blush. Why does it always sound sexual? "How expressive you were. I could really get that you were in your character's situation. You know, fighting for what you believe in."

He laughs a little bit. His permanent marker swings and loops around over his bio in the program. When he's done signing, he flips back through pictures, action shots of the play. "I love the role," he says. "Sorry, I would say more, but . . ."

"No, it's okay," I blurt out. "You obviously need to rest your voice. In your line of work, I can't imagine anything more important."

Alec nods, and as if on cue, the kettle whistles. He pours boiling water into a mug with a waiting teabag and squeezes an ungodly amount of honey into it from a bear-shaped bottle. He sips it slowly, wincing in discomfort. I kind of feel like I should leave, but he hasn't handed back my program yet, so I wait, fidgeting awkwardly.

He sighs, looking at a picture in the program where he's perched atop the barricade, musket in hand, eyes fiery and mouth open wide in song. "I can't believe I got this part," he says. "I never expected anything so professional so soon. There are so many more qualified actors than me here, and if—" His voice squeaks and he stops. He sips more of his honey solution. His eyes are the opposite of fiery now: full of worry. "If my voice gives out," he whispers, "it could all be over before it begins."

I just stand there, arms hanging uselessly at my sides. I feel like I weigh a million pounds.

"Well, I think you're fantastic," I say. "Take care of your voice and you'll do great."

He nods and finally hands back my program. "If only it were that easy."

I leave the room. He closes the door.

Jesus. Talk about a killjoy. Talk about broken dreams. My expectations are like a shattered ornament, beautiful only in hindsight.

On top of the abrupt, heavy sadness, I'm also hopelessly lost. I try fumbling my way toward the stage, but it's all completely dark. Stagehands pack away props and actors are laughing and undressed and obviously on their way somewhere else. How do I get back to the stage? I'm too scared to ask the many busy, clipboard-toting people, since I'm pretty sure I'm not really supposed to be here. When my wandering and fumbling proves to be fruitless, I just use the nearest door marked EXIT.

It dumps me out into an alley. Theatre people line the brick walls, smoking and laughing shrilly. I clutch my sweater around myself and head up the alley toward the front doors.

But the theatre lobby is dark. I tug on the doors. They're locked.

Levi is nowhere to be seen.

"Levi?" I glance around the street. People mill about, but I don't see my hulking brother anywhere.

I pound on the lobby doors.

"Hey, you!" I call at an usher walking past. "I lost somebody! Hey, help!"

He barely glances at me as he walks past.

Tears start to choke me. I pound harder on the glass, but it's probably pointless.

"Help," I whisper. "Help, help, help."

No one comes to my rescue. I stay pressed against the glass doors for a small eternity, hoping and praying that some solution will pop out of thin air. Maybe some Parisian magic will spark along this darkening street and the ghost of Victor Hugo or something will lead me to my brother.

No magic. No solution. Only me, paralyzed and cowering.

I guess I have to make my own magic.

I pick a direction and stride purposefully up the street. Maybe I can fool myself into believing that I'm a strong young woman capable of dealing with this situation. I try to think like a detective. Where would Levi go? He knows I was coming to get him, so he wouldn't stray too far. There's no familiar landmark around he might have been drawn to, and he certainly wouldn't ask a stranger for directions.

Why the hell didn't he just stay close to the theatre? He knew I was coming back, why didn't he just wait for me?

I'm wondering if I should maybe turn and go the other direction when I round a corner and see a bright light across the way: McDonald's. Levi is a big lumpy silhouette in the front window. I swear I almost evacuate my bowels in relief.

I hurry across and wrench open the door. It's bright, friendly, full of primary colors. Levi turns to me as I walk in.

"Where the fuck were you?" he says. "They kicked me out, you took so long."

"Where were *you?* I came out and you were just fucking gone! Why didn't you just wait out front or something, somewhere I could easily find you?"

He shrugs moodily. "I'm hungry."

I sigh and go for my wallet. I'm still clutching my autographed program. I tuck it safely into my purse.

"I need chicken nuggets," he says. "And a large fry and large Coke."

I buy his food and a couple of cheeseburgers for myself—worrying really burns through a stomach full of crêpes—and we eat in silence. My heart is still recovering from the fear of finding Levi gone. How did we ever get to this point? How could my adorable baby brother, who called me Kee-wa until only a few years ago, become so fragile, so close to the edge of nonexistence? *Levi is right here*, I try to convince myself. *Levi is with me. Safe.*

I can't believe I got so distracted. There's no way Alec Rideout could have lived up to the fantasy I fabricated. No one ever does; haven't I already learned that lesson? *Family before boys.* I need FBB on a bracelet to remind me.

I repeat it like a mantra inside my head, feeling a little comforted.

I swear I won't need to learn this lesson a third time.

# Chapter Twelve

The next day, Levi's monotone wakes me up. "Keira, we have to go to that bakery again."

You don't need to ask me twice.

The day is gorgeous. Warm, even in the early morning, and sunny as a tropical paradise. The bakery is full of the light that reflects off our hotel's windows—and full to bursting with treats.

We pick mostly the same things we had yesterday, but today there's an even bigger menagerie of tiny marzipan animals under the glass. Little elephants and pigs, even cows with tiny blobby spots. I get one of each, as well as an unhealthy amount of croissants and jam cookies.

Levi discovers he doesn't like marzipan, so I get all the animals to myself. No problem. We polish off everything and then I fan the brochures out across the tabletop.

Levi leans forward, his lower lip puckered in concentration. He grabs my metro map and surveys it. "Franklin D. Roosevelt," he murmurs, pointing out that same stop. "Funny."

I let him pick what he wants to do today, and he's obviously going to take forever, so I lean back in my chair to admire the shop. Okay, and to give my stomach room to shamelessly expand. I didn't notice the old photographs on the walls yesterday, shots of a family in bellbottoms and wide collars, in what might be this very shop. When I've digested my food, I stand up to examine the pictures further.

"*Ma famille*," the woman behind the counter says, the same lady from yesterday. Her eyes sparkle with pride. "I am in the middle, five years old. My brother on the left side. He is chef here."

I smile at her. "That's so cool. Is this your . . . grandfather?"

She nods, beaming.

"He used to own this building," she says. "He used to have a *pâtisserie* in this building, too. But the business was lost in the occupation."

"Occupation?" I put it all together in my head, luckily before she has to explain to the American moron. "Oh, the Nazi Occupation."

"*Oui*." Her perpetual smile fades a little. "I save up for many years to buy these premises and restart the family business."

Whoa. "That's . . . that's amazing."

The smile is back. "*Merci. C'est ce que je crois, aussi.*"

*That's what I believe, too.*

A man in a white chef's outfit, who looks exactly like the woman—he could only be her brother—emerges from the kitchen. He has the same unbeatable smile.

"*On a besoin de quelque chose?*" he asks. "*Des croissants, plus de pain?*"

*Do we need anything? Croissants, more bread?* His sister glances at us and glances toward the door. The shop is empty.

"*Non*," she says quietly, shaking her head.

In the time it's taken to have my heart broken by the pastry chefs, Levi still hasn't decided on a plan for the day.

"Pick something," I say, tapping his arm. "War stuff?"

He shrugs. Perilously noncommittal. "We already looked at guns and stuff yesterday."

"If you aren't going to pick something, I will."

He pushes the brochures at me. I take this as permission to do whatever the hell I want. And as soon as I see the corner of the brochure poking out from all the rest, I've decided.

We're going to Versailles today.

⁂

Versailles. Finally, Versailles. I'll be walking the halls Marie Antoinette walked, seeing myself reflected in the Hall of Mirrors. I'll be in my dingy travel clothes, not the eighteenth-century garb of my dreams—not even my imitation Marie Antoinette prom dress—but it's still my dream, the stereotypical princess fantasy that I'm not ashamed to admit I've always had. That, and my dream of going back in time and whisking Marie Antoinette off to a time that would have been kinder to her.

Versailles is just a forty-five-minute tour bus ride from the center of Paris. We disembark from the bus into the biggest parking lot I've ever seen, and on the other side is the palace, a planetary-sized building, all pillars and huge picture windows, statues of cherubs and saints adorning the roof. I can almost smell the grandeur. The other tourists on our bus flock toward the gates. I hang back to take a picture. I can barely fit the whole palace in one shot.

"This is the first picture I've taken here," I laugh, snapping the photo. "It's going to look like we arrived here straight off the plane."

Levi doesn't say anything. He just stares at the palace, squinting in the sun, with an otherwise neutral expression.

"Lev? What do you think?"

He shrugs.

I'm not going to let his indifference ruin this. This is *Versailles*.

We start the long walk up to the gilded gates, and the closer we get, the worse my stomach ache gets. It's like I'm about to be introduced to a celebrity crush I've lusted after for years. Back at home, I have hundreds of pictures on my computer's hard drive of frescoed walls, gold-foiled crown moldings, and the magnificent gardens. I'd pump Jacques for information and descriptions of the palace. He never said much, just kind of brushed me off. Later, I guess when the novelty of me fawning over him wore off, he admitted to me that he'd never even been inside the palace, even though he *lives in Versailles.*

Far across the massive parking lot, I can see the houses and restaurants of the town of Versailles. I don't see any houses like Jacques described, row houses with flower boxes at the windows, but I can see them in my head when I close my eyes. Jacques and Selena could be there together right now, wearing black turtle necks and berets, giggling to each other.

I clench my fists. That used to be all I ever wanted, to come home with Jacques. Not really because of him—sometimes I used him like he used me. No, I wanted the free place to stay, the link to this place. A starting point. A diving board. Selena could be perched at the end of that diving board now, about to jump into everything I've ever wanted. Meanwhile, I just paid an exorbitant amount for a ride on a shitty bus to stand in this lineup for an hour.

Just when I feel like I'm miles from my dream, I look up. The Palace's two wings cradle me in the *Court Royale*; their columns, gilded details, and busts of eminent characters seem to smile down at me.

I'm here.

Levi fidgets beside me.

"Thank you for being so patient," I tell him. "We'll be inside soon."

"And then it's just going to be more standing around," he says, and the instant he lets one negative thought out of his mouth, it unleashes the flood. "It's just going to be more portraits of rich people and paintings by dead guys and idiots staring at them. Ugh, I can't even believe you wanted to come here."

"It's *Versailles*."

"How can you even like the French monarchy?" His glare is stormier than the sky. "They were fucking terrible."

When he says stuff like that, starts on political diatribes grown from the pro-Communism websites he trolls, I get this "shut up, Levi" knee-jerk feeling, and a million possible arguments could break the surface, but I stifle them all because he'll start using that damn circular logic and I'll end up so mad I can't breathe, let alone argue properly. The whole thing just makes me hate him. And I don't want to hate him, especially not here, in the shadow of Versailles, under the watchful gaze of windows Marie Antoinette once peered out. Here, I just want to feel wonder and that old sadness. But Levi won't let me.

"You know Marie Antoinette was an idiot, right?" he says.

"Oh God, Levi, just stop," I groan.

"Why? You don't know her. She isn't, like, your ancestor or anything. Why do you even care?"

I can't even begin to explain it to him. No matter what I say, he won't understand the overwhelming sympathy I feel for her, a young girl uprooted from her country and married off to another, barely knowing the language when she arrived. Having to figure out the rules in a new court. Dealing with an arranged, loveless marriage, never mind the enormous, constant scrutiny that that marriage was under. And then, later, having to deal with the people of France completely turning on her family and sending them, unapologetically, to their deaths.

"You know she was probably illiterate, right? And she didn't care about the people at all. She was totally up her own ass."

"None of that is her fault," I say, measuring each word.

Levi makes a disgusted face. "She didn't even try to investigate what the life of the average citizen was like. She just lazed around this place all day, letting her servants do everything for her."

"She was aristocratically born and bred. She never knew the life of a commoner; she was purposefully kept ignorant. That isn't her fault."

"She could've tried."

"Levi, would it be reasonable of me to freak out at you for not understanding the plight of the three-toed sloth? Or the humpback whale? Or any other form of life that is anything other than a teenaged boy?"

He glares, but not at me. At the windows, at the tourists in line with us.

"She just wanted to sit around all day," he says. "With nice, expensive things around her all the time, doing nothing."

I groan. So much for trying to force some perspective on him.

"You don't know anything."

"Keira, *you* don't know anything."

I fold my arms across my chest. He's got me there, but at least I'm a little less stubborn than an old mule. "Whatever. Let's just go inside and look at all her nice, expensive things."

His glare gets even cloudier but he doesn't say anything.

And thank God. Because once we're inside, underneath a frescoed ceiling that feels like it covers a square mile, I don't want to hear Levi's venomous voice grumbling about how it took so much out of the artist to paint that he killed himself after its completion. I shell out for the audio tour headset so I can tune out his pessimism and tune into cheesy, tinkling harpsichord music and an English gentleman feeding me tidbits of information.

Each room just kind of leads into the next, shrinking as they go. There are no real hallways or corridors. Back in the day, there were guards at each door, deciding who could and couldn't advance into the next room. The public was allowed in the palace, allowed to roam free, for the most part, through the courtyards and outer rooms. You had to be a little fancier to get a little further in, and it got more and more selective until only a privileged few could enter the smaller rooms and have more chance of being alone with the king and queen.

In the Queen's Bedroom, I picture Marie Antoinette walking these floors. Sleeping in that bed (sometimes). Having to give birth in that bed, in front of the gawking public—what a nightmare—so that no one could dispute a royal birth. She lived a good portion of her life with no privacy, with her cottage in the vast gardens as her only escape. I can hear Levi now, complaining about how silly it was that an adult woman, a queen, played peasant in the woods. The epitome of First World Problems: too much money, too much privilege, so you run off and play pauper every once in a while.

I get it, though. It wasn't the money or the privilege she was trying to escape; it was her own life. The perfection was an illusion; palace equaled prison. She probably built it all up in her mind when she was married at fifteen—she was going to be the queen of France! Everything was going to be brilliant and perfect forever! She could never have imagined the constant, unceasing criticism, the horrible marriage, the contrived charges and the bloody execution.

Ideal situations don't always turn out like you expect.

As understandable as that is, my inner cynic—my inner Levi—starts getting snarky. All these mammoth portraits taking up whole walls, frescoes on ceilings painted by masters, cabinets and candlesticks and tchotchkes made of gold and gems . . . it all seems false. Pointless. Meaningless. Because really, why is it all here? To satisfy the vanities of a select few? What good does that do? These objects made from precious resources at such high cost, serving no material purpose. I can't find the part of me that just reveled in glory without a second thought. Suddenly I'm mercenary, utilitarian, staring up at a chandelier so dripping with crystals that I can't even see where the candles would go and wondering what the fuck the point is. Yeah, maybe she had a sad, boxed-in life, the same way some celebrities have sad, boxed-in lives, but all this glittering gold and crystal, here purely to tickle her fancy and trick lesser beings into worship? It's senseless.

This place isn't a shrine to beauty. It's an exhibit of hopelessness.

The rest of the palace passes in a haze of disappointment, directed at myself. I dream of this place forever, and then when I finally arrive, I give in to Levi's pessimism. I look at marble pillars and wish they were stone, I look up at gilded moldings and think *too elaborate*. But I can't even mourn. I'm tired.

The rear of the palace faces onto the enormous grounds. The (artificial) lake goes on forever into the distance. Scale and size, that's what these places are about. That's *all* they're about.

I pull out my map of the grounds and find the star that marks Marie Antoinette's private estate. I've always wanted to see her cottage, but now, somehow, it doesn't mean anything to me. Has part of me died? I've misplaced my sympathy for her.

Levi starts to back away from the gardens, toward the exit. I look over my shoulder at the man-made lake and sculpted, manicured gardens, the promise of *ooh*s and *ahh*s and that little thrill of a feeling, deep in my chest, when something beautiful touches me just so. Once upon a time, all I ever wanted . . .

I walk back to the bus.

The bus ride into the city center is fraught with existential crap. Versailles was impressive, of course, but empty. I essentially met my celebrity crush, and he was a complete asshole.

I think about taking Marie Antoinette off the list in my head of girls I would save if I had a time machine. Sure, there are men I would go back and save, but infinitely more women. Women had all the tragedies and deserved almost none of them. Anne Boleyn. Joan of Arc. Olga, Tatiana, Maria, and Anastasia Romanov. Anne Frank. Marie Antoinette was always on that list. Her beheading seemed like the cruelest thing in the world. She was beautiful and innocent and, I thought, a martyr, and the world cut her down with a sharp blade to the neck. Now I think Levi might be right: sure, she stood for beauty and unadulterated fun, but she was ignorant, sheltered, and not even very intelligent. A selfish, silly little girl.

But I'm selfish and silly a lot of the time. Does that mean I deserve a bloody execution? Does that mean I'm not worth saving?

"If you could go back in time and rescue someone," I say to Levi as we hurtle along the highway back to Paris, "someone who suffered a fate they didn't deserve, who would you save?"

Levi is quiet for a long time. He stares out at the trees we pass with his lips pressed tightly together.

"Hitler," he says.

A few seconds pass before I recover enough to respond. "Hitler. Adolf Hitler."

"No, Joe Hitler. Of course, Adolf. He was brilliant. Good leader. Good planner, aside from the war-on-two-fronts thing, and the Russian winter thing. And he was an artist."

"Jesus Christ, Levi, he killed millions of people!"

"Not personally," Levi counters.

"*Technicality.*"

"Way more people died at the hands of Stalin."

"So I'm guessing you'd save him, too."

"No. He was evil."

I roll my eyes, but seriously, what the fuck. Does my brother *really* sympathize with Hitler? Isn't that illegal? Maybe I should text Mom. She's worried before about him getting into weird shit. Nazi shit would definitely qualify.

"You just said to pick someone to save," he says. "You didn't say save from their death. What if I choose to save someone from their life?"

Nothing comes out when I open my mouth. Levi keeps going.

"What if Hitler was accepted to art school in Vienna? What if he never joined the military or fell on hard times? What if he never had the chance to develop a hatred for Jews? What if he just quietly studied art and went on to sell paintings and just lived out the rest of his life harmlessly?"

Holy crap, I think he might be kind of right. I run the theory through my brain and, somehow, it all makes sense. What if we could neutralize the harm in people like Hitler?

Maybe Hitler could have a spot—if I can come to terms with the fact that the name Adolf Hitler would appear on any list containing my favorite people from history.

"That's very wise of you, Levi," I tell him.

He shrugs. "It's just logic. Who would you save?"

He's probably just going to rip me apart for all my choices, but I tell him anyway.

"Anne Boleyn, because Henry VIII was a brute. Joan of Arc, for obvious reasons. Olga, Tatiana, Maria, and Anastasia Romanov."

"So basically every princess ever."

"Well, princesses were so often used as pawns. But Joan of Arc was the opposite of a princess."

"Wait, who was she again?"

"The French girl who heard voices she thought were angels telling her to lead the French army against England. She was burned at the stake for heresy, but really just because she wore men's clothes and challenged peoples' assumptions of what a poor, illiterate girl could do."

"Speaking of illiterate girls, is Marie Antoinette on your list?" he sneers.

"She was," I say, sighing. "But maybe you're right. Maybe in another context, she would've just been a silly, average girl."

"So she deserved to get her head chopped off via guillotine?"

"Well, no, but . . . wait, you switched opinions!"

Levi shrugs, biting his thumbnail. "Just trying to make you think."

I don't know what to think. I just kind of look at him for a while as he gnaws his nails and stares out the window, and I feel something I don't often feel for Levi: pride. My little brother is an interesting, unique person. Maybe he says weird things sometimes—weird, sorta-pro-Nazi things—but they're weird things that come from pure intelligence.

Even when Lego and PlayMobil were the order of the day, I had this vague worry that Levi would slip through the cracks. Levi had a pretty bad speech impediment when he was little, he always wore those rain boots and sweatpants in the summer, and he was known to switch to shorts and sandals in the snow. Now that he's older, he lets his scraggly facial hair take over his face and refuses to replace his crooked glasses. He still doesn't speak to strangers, and he considers everyone but Mom and me to be strangers. The world tends not to treat people like him very kindly, and even when I was young, I was afraid for him. Afraid the world would stop trying to reach him, because he refused to be reached.

Then on this average day during junior year, I left my English class to go to the bathroom, and on my way there, I passed by an open classroom door and heard Levi's voice. I peeked inside. It was his freshman history class and he was giving a PowerPoint presentation. His voice was loud—almost too loud, like he didn't know how to control it. He stood there crookedly, clicking the remote to switch slides, his other arm tucked against his tummy like a wing, in that way he has. But none of that mattered. He was talking about the Bolsheviks, not even looking at his slides, no cue cards in his hand. All the facts were memorized, but the words were off the cuff. He was just speaking his mind. And his classmates were listening intently. His teacher smiled behind her hand, like this side of him was brand new to her, too.

I grinned on my way to the bathroom. It was the first time I had felt reassurance when it came to Levi. The first time I felt that he could make it.

I try to forget the fear and constant worry of the past two months, Dr. Pearson erasing all hope, because right now I feel it again: he'll be okay someday.

# Chapter Thirteen

In the morning, Levi refuses to get out of bed. I get dressed and cross the street to our bakery. Maybe fresh bread can wake him up. And croissants, and cookies, and marzipan animals . . .

I tug on the door handle but it doesn't budge. The store is dark. The glass case that holds all the miraculously delicious things is empty.

I glance at my phone to check the time—maybe I'm ridiculously early?—when the date jumps out at me. Sunday, August 30. Sunday.

Everyone is Catholic and in church today.

While I'm still standing there, probably looking desperate, the woman who runs the bakery emerges from a door behind the counter, in pajamas. She's looking for something around the cash register when she glances up and sees me. She rushes to open the door.

"*Ma chérie, je suis désolé,* we are closed!" she exclaims.

"I know, I just realized," I say with a laugh, my cheeks starting to burn. I must look so stupid. "We'll have to find something else."

"No, there is nothing open," she says. "*Reviens!* Come back in one hour. I will make your breakfast."

I try to protest, but she won't take no for an answer. She bustles off, saying she must get her lazy brother on his feet and baking as soon as he opens his eyes.

I'm as selfish as Marie Antoinette. I'm ecstatic at the prospect of freshly baked goods, made just for me, on a lazy Sunday morning. I feel horrible for disturbing them, too, but come on. Those croissants.

I go back to the hotel and wake Levi, telling him about our luck. "Isn't that nice of her?" I say as he yawns cavernously. "We'll have to think of something to do for her in return."

"Why aren't they open on Sundays?" he asks.

Oh boy. He hates religion.

"A lot of people in France are Catholic."

"They're just lazy," he scoffs. "All businesses should be open all day. Twenty-four hours, if feasible. It's the most convenient."

"Not for the people who you would have work twenty-four hours a day, seven days a week."

"Uh, it's called working shifts." He frowns in irritation.

"I'll pass on your business advice to the entire working world, then."

If he hears the sarcasm in my voice, he doesn't acknowledge it.

We get dressed and go down to the bakery. The woman ushers us in with her big smile and shows us to our usual table.

"Sit, sit! The croissants are ready. The rest will be ready soon."

"The rest?" I repeat. "You didn't bake us the entire works, did you?"

"Only a few things," she says with a wave of her hand.

She won't let me say another word. She brings us a plate of croissants drizzled with chocolate, still steaming. Their buttery flakes call to me like the One Ring calls to Sauron.

The owner, nothing to do since her business is not actually open, putters around the front counter at first, but ends up pulling up a chair at our table. I push the plate of croissants toward her. She smiles shyly.

"Oh, I could not."

"Of course. Please, have some."

"Well . . ." She reaches for a smaller croissant. "Nico does bake the best."

"The best I've ever had," I say, and then I realize something. "I'm sorry, I can't believe I don't know your names."

She blushes. "*Je m'appelle* Margot Belliveau. My brother is Nico."

"*Je m'appelle* Keira Braidwood," I say, holding out my hand. She shakes it. "*Mon frère s'appelle* Levi."

"*C'est merveilleux de vous recontrez*," she says.

"*Et vous*," I answer. "This is the exact conversation I had on the first day of French 101. It's uncanny."

She laughs and it's like bells.

Levi sits through all of this with a slight frown on his face as he chows down on croissants. He shoves a little too much into his mouth at a time. I really hope Margot doesn't notice.

"*Il parle français?*" she asks me, indicating Levi.

I shake my head and whisper, "He barely speaks English when it comes to strangers."

She chuckles. "Nico is almost the same. In fact . . . Nico?"

I decide that I love that name, especially the way she says it: not NEE-co, but ni-CO. Somehow it makes a world of difference.

"*Oui?*" Nico emerges from the kitchen wearing a purple button-down and gray pants dusted with flour. Not his usual baking clothes, I'd imagine. He has his sister's glowing cheeks perched on high cheekbones, and his eyes show signs of early crow's feet; he's definitely a smiler, too. Just not in uncertain company.

"*Voici* Keira *et* Levi Braidwood," Margot says.

He nods. "*Salut.*"

"*Bonjour*," I say. Levi says nothing.

"*Merci pour* . . . uh . . . all this," I gesticulate around the croissants. "*Merci beaucoup.*"

"*De rien.*" *It's nothing.* Nico smiles shyly. "*Les biscuits suivent.*"

*Cookies are next.* My mouth waters all over again.

"What are you two doing today?" Margot asks. "A beautiful Sunday. So many choices."

"I don't know," I say, looking at Levi. "We went to Versailles yesterday."

"Ahh, *magnifique*," she says. "You enjoyed it?"

It seems too heavy to say I had an existential crisis at Versailles. So I just nod and say it was beautiful.

"You must go to the *Tour Eiffel* today," Margot says simply. "The day is perfect for that."

*Yes.*

"What do you think?" I ask Levi. "Eiffel Tower?"

Chewing on one of the hot cookies Nico just brought out, Levi nods. "Have to finish these first," he says, stuffing another one into his mouth.

I turn to Margot. This is my chance to maybe do something for them. "Would you like to come with us? I mean, I'm sure you've seen the Eiffel Tower thousands of times, but . . . my treat, as a thank-you for breakfast?"

"Oh!" Margot flaps her hands. "Oh, I could not. Your money!"

"Please?" I beg. "I mean, I understand if you have somewhere to go or something. But if you don't, and Nico doesn't, we'd love for you to come."

She considers it for a moment and looks back at the kitchen.

"Nico?"

"*Oui?*"

"*Tour Eiffel?*"

He pokes his head out and looks at her quizzically. "*Toi?*" he asks. *You?*

"*Et toi*," she adds. *And you.*

He ducks back into the kitchen and calls, "I will get my coat."

Sunday may be dead in the *13e arrondissement*, but the Eiffel Tower, in the *1ière arrondissement*, is teeming with life. The long grassy park leading to the tower, the Champs de Mars, is full of tourists enjoying the sunlight and taking photos of them pretending to lean against the tower. Voices giggle and shout in Japanese, Spanish, Hindi, Russian—every language I could name and many I couldn't if I tried.

The Eiffel Tower has been a far-off watcher and reminder, but now it's so in-your-face we couldn't ignore it if we wanted to.

"Same height as an eighty-one story building, you know," Nico tells us.

"That seems impossible," I say, laughing.

"Of course it's not, moron," Levi murmurs beside me.

I swat at his arm. He flaps his hand back at me.

Margot points at the camera around my neck as we stroll down the Champs de Mars. "I can take a photo of you two, if you wish?"

I hand Margot the camera. I only have a handful of half-hearted pictures. This trip is going to end sooner rather than later, and I know I'm going to regret not having photographic evidence.

Margot arranges Levi and I with a few feet between us and shoots from a cross-legged position on the ground. She snaps the pictures and grins.

"You both are giants."

I look at the picture on the little display. It's a bad angle for me; I have about three extra chins. I sure look happy, though, pretending to lean against the Eiffel Tower. Levi's hand is out like he's poking it, like a total goof, but his face is impassive. I laugh.

"Mom would love this picture," I say, showing him. "We should take more, really silly ones."

Levi grunts. I look around for a photo op.

"There! Go stand by those pigeons." Levi does, dragging his feet along the pavement. "Now do something funny."

"What do you mean, do something funny?" he grumbles. He waves his arms in the air, making a face. "Like this?"

I snap the picture, and when I turn the camera around, I start laughing like a madwoman. Levi stands in a crowd of pigeons, arms thrown wildly over his head. His eyes are crossed and his tongue sticks out.

"This is the best you've ever looked in a picture," I tell him. When he sees it, he grunts, but that's it.

We continue on to the tower. The square it stands on is Tokyo-subway-level crowded. Here, you can only see the top of the tower if you look up, way up, so far you have to bend backward. You never see it in pictures, but huge swaths of netting stretch from each of the tower's four legs to catch any suicidal jumpers. Good thing, too—the ground teems with tourists. Imagining a jumper going *ker-splat* in the middle of all that chaos is pretty brutal. I almost open my mouth to say this to Levi, but then I remember being woken in the middle of the night. Ambulances. Levi kept prisoner for two months.

My heart squeezes tight. I can't think about that, not now, when I'm about to ascend the equivalent of eighty-one stories.

"We take the elevator, right?" Margot asks, pointing to two lines, one to buy tickets for the elevator, one to buy tickets to walk up.

I always had this romantic vision of myself climbing each step on the Eiffel Tower. It seemed a more authentic, pure experience. But now all I can think is nope, nope, nope. It is way higher than I'd pictured in my head. Even the first level is squint-to-see-details high.

"Elevator," I say definitively.

Margot looks relieved.

It takes a long time to get onto the elevator. I expect Levi to complain and fidget and whine, but he stays remarkably quiet. I worry that this is just a sign of an impending implosion, but when I try to get him to talk—"Look at that dog! That guy's hair is funny. Ooh, look, a mime!"—he responds pretty well. By "pretty well," I mean that his grunts slant up instead of down.

I take a bunch more pictures of us making faces, sticking our tongues so close to metal poles and rope dividers that it looks like we're licking them, and then I take a series of photos I have titled "Levi Coughing in Various Locales." I tell him to go over to a tree and cough under it. Cough next to the mammoth leg of the Eiffel Tower. Cough against a background of tourists crowding together making peace signs. In every picture, Levi is just standing there, face all scrunched up, a fist in front of his mouth. For some reason, it's hilarious. I laugh like I did that time in Walmart with the romance novels.

We finally get into the elevator. They pack it pretty tight, but I make sure Levi has plenty of space near the window. He tilts his head to examine the massive cables the elevator slides along.

"Huh," he says. "The elevator goes up diagonally. Makes sense, I guess. Since the legs are slanted."

I get a wibbly-wobbly feeling in the pit of my stomach, and it gets worse when the elevator starts to move. It's smooth and safe-feeling, but the angle freaks me out. We are moving diagonally, higher and higher, but also sideways. The combination of directions makes me woozy. I close my eyes and grip the handlebar under the window until the elevator comes to a stop. I open my eyes and pretend I'm still on ground level as we exit.

And it almost feels like we *are* still on ground level, if the wind at ground level had ripped at our clothes and whistled this angrily. If the view from ground level stood way, way above the treetops and you could see the Montparnasse Tower in the distance, the only thing anywhere near as tall as the Eiffel Tower.

So, not ground level at all, basically.

We're on solid ground, though, and far away from any railings. The crowds are still enormous, with people bustling to and from the gift shop and the—wait.

"Is there a restaurant on the Eiffel Tower?" I ask Margot, pointing in the direction of a doorway where a hostess stands, smiling at a group approaching.

"There are two," she says, laughing.

Somehow I missed that in all my research. The tower is like its own island, self-sustaining. You could stay on it forever.

"You need months in advance for the reservation," Nico says. "But I hear the food is very good."

I don't think I could eat this high up if I tried. Levi, however, is fine. Hands in his hoodie pocket, just looking around.

"Let's go to the second level now," he says after we wander for a few minutes.

"You don't want to go to the gift shop? No Eiffel Tower keychains for you?"

"There're guys selling them on the ground."

"We should get some for Mom and Josh and everyone back home."

He nods. "Let's buy them on the ground, though. You should only make purchases on the ground."

I can't figure out if this is one of his weird logical hang-ups, or if he's using some made-up metaphor for not making purchases with your head in the clouds.

"Okay, Levi," I say, patting his arm.

We find the elevator to take us to the second floor. I can't imagine, now, walking up the stairs to this point, attaining this insane height slowly, slowly, slowly, your legs aching after carrying you up 1,700 steps, higher than any building in the city center of Paris. It's better—less scary, more sane and rational—to take the elevator. Pure, authentic experience or not.

The elevator to the third and final floor is cramped. Levi and I get wedged behind a mother holding the hand of a little boy, maybe three or four years old. While the mom talks to her friend in French, the little boy sneaks an Eiffel Tower keychain into his mouth. His mom gasps and pulls it out.

"What did I tell you?" she scolds him in French.

"*On ne met pas le Tour Eiffel dans la bouche*," he recites miserably.

I cover my mouth to keep from laughing. *We don't put the Eiffel Tower in our mouths*, recited in perfectly accented French by a tiny child voice.

"Why are you laughing?" Levi asks.

I point to the boy and whisper, "His little French accent is so perfect."

"Hilarious," Levi deadpans.

The elevator lurches into motion.

I clutch Levi's hand tightly.

We.

Are.

So.

High.

They never really say it when they talk about the Eiffel Tower. Oh, it's beautiful, it's a symbol of the great nation of France, it's a marvel of engineering, blah, blah, blah. What you'll never hear them say is "holy fucking shit, those clouds look awfully close."

The top floor is just an observation deck. It's completely fenced in, absolutely no risk of falling or jumping—although part of me is a little disappointed there's no ledge you could teeter across. Only because I once read a (horribly researched, I now realize) novel where the eccentric love interest cart-wheeled along the edge of the Eiffel Tower's top floor. That romantic, death-defying image is wiped away forever.

But forget the fantasy—the real top of the Eiffel Tower is magnificent.

You can see for literal miles in all directions. The hill of Montmartre, with the beautiful white edifice of Sacré Coeur perched at the top. L'Arc de Triomphe, in the middle of a distant roundabout. The Louvre, the dome of the Pantheon, the glass of the Musée d'Orsay. It's all here. And, so distant it looks two-dimensional, like a painting, I can see Notre Dame. Waiting for me.

Forget Versailles. The Eiffel Tower and this view are where it's at.

I stand at the handrail and stare out at the city for a long, long time. The wind whips my hair all over; anyone standing within a meter is in danger of getting a mouthful. Levi looks at the inside of the observation deck rather than at the view. He grabs the cage surrounding us and tries to shake it. Of course, it doesn't move.

"Sturdy," he says. "Good."

"If it wasn't, the wind would blow us back to Seattle," I laugh.

"Look." Levi points behind us into a foggy glass window. There's a little room with a creepy mannequin set up at a big old-fashioned radio set in a military uniform.

"It was radio outpost in early part of the war."

I turn when Nico speaks. He peers into the little room, too, smiling mildly at the mannequin.

"It'd be crazy to be stationed up here," I say. "So lonely."

"Yes, my grandfather said it was lonely. Only the radio for company."

"Your grandfather? He worked the radio here?"

He nods. "In the beginning. Before Occupation."

"That's so cool," I say. "Do you come here a lot? Did he ever bring you here?"

He just shakes his head and starts to wander away. I don't know if he meant no to one question or both. Levi wanders away, too, examining the floor with his arms tucked up to his stomach.

I find Margot tracing an oval fingernail over the many initials and graffitied messages in the handrail.

"Nico just told me your grandfather worked in that little room as a radio operator," I say.

She nods, smiling her friendly smile. "*Il vivait une vie incroyable*," she says. *He lived an incredible life.*

Margot is quiet for a long time. I watch Levi a few feet away as he looks out at the city, hands in his hoodie pockets. I hope he isn't too cold.

"I told you my *grandpère* had the bakery in our building now," she says.

I nod.

"That was before the war. He shut down to work for French Resistance. He hid Jewish neighbors in the bakery." She squints, looking out at the view, but there's unrest behind her eyes as she sweeps them over the horizon, as her grandfather must have done.

"Wow," I breathe. "That's . . . pretty amazing. Did they . . . were they . . .?"

"Sent to a camp, *oui*. *Grandpère*, too."

I shiver, but not from the cold wind. "He survived, right?"

She dabs at her nose with a tissue from her pocket. She folds it up many times before nodding slowly. "He was never the same," she says. "Well, of course, I did not know him before. But *Grandmère*, she told me the stories of how he used to be."

"The building, was it passed down through your family? The bakery?"

She shakes her head. "It fell into disrepair during the rest of the Occupation and eventually the building sells. Nico and I, we bought it back. We start our bakery, to honor *Grandpère*."

My heart melts.

"But . . ." Margot's hand flutters over her mouth and she closes her eyes. "*J'ai peur qu'on ne va pas réussir.*"

"What?" She's afraid they won't . . . I don't recognize the last word. "What do you mean?"

"The business is new, but we struggle." Her voice wobbles. "No one needs another *pâtisserie*. But baking, it is our passion, we could not do anything else. The people, they walk past our shop and look, only looking, no buying, no visiting. I want to tell them about my grandfather and the Jews who lived in our kitchen in secret. Maybe it will make them buy. But I cannot. It would be too . . . taking advantage of . . ." She waves her hand and looks at me, pleading for me to understand.

"Too . . . exploitative?" I try. She looks perplexed. "Like you're exploiting the tragedy to make money?"

"Yes, yes, *c'est ça*. I could not. I could never."

I disappoint myself by falling silent. Offering no words of encouragement, no words of comfort. No helpful, practical suggestions, even, because I'm just a kid, and what do I really know about running a business? Margot and Nico's baking would sell itself, in a perfect world, and make them millionaires. But our world is far, far from perfect. Ours is a world where a man tries to save his neighbors and is sent to prison and has his livelihood sold off and the rest of his years ruined.

Worry settles into a pit in my stomach. This is my vacation and I don't *have* to worry about any of this, but I can't help it. They're such sweet people, and their family story deserves to be told. They deserve to have that bald guy walk into their shop and buy his daily croissant from them instead of passing by.

Nico and Levi stand together now. Nico points out Les Invalides to Levi. I see his mouth form the words "We went there." My stomach flutters; he's talking to another living person.

"Your brother, *il est différent*," Margot says. *He's different.* She doesn't ask. She knows.

I nod. "He's sick. Or so they think."

"You are not sure?"

"I just think there's more than that," I admit. "His whole personality can't come from something that can be killed with medicine. He isn't just a walking disease."

"Keira," she says, touching my arm. "He can be himself and still be sick. My *grandpère* was a quiet man, he would never be a loud man, but things he saw in the war, in the camps . . . they made him sick."

I watch Levi mutter a few more words in answer to Nico.

"Maybe," I say.

A huge gust of wind rockets through the observation deck, making everyone close their eyes. I start laughing, the way you do when you're scared shitless. The hysterical laugh of a terrified person.

# Chapter Fourteen

"Would you like to go to Notre Dame?" Margot asks when we're back on the ground. "I would like to light a candle for *Grandpère*."

I can't pass it up.

The metro ride is calm and soothing, as is the walk over a bridge to the Isle de la Cité, the "island of the city." Margot and I talk about the *Hunchback of Notre Dame* Disney movie, which she likes, and the Victor Hugo novel it was based on, which she loves. I admit to her that I've always wanted to read it, in the original French, but was too intimidated.

She nods thoughtfully. "I feel the same about many English novels. Translation is not the same."

Exactly.

Looking at pictures of Notre Dame and standing under the towering spectacle of it are worlds, galaxies, *universes* apart. The city began with Notre Dame at its heart, spreading outward from here. I can feel the weight of all those years. I can feel the thousands of souls who have been here before humming inside me. There's history everywhere, whether or not there are surviving buildings, but there's something different about a place full of structures that have stood for hundreds of years, approaching a millennium. Knowing that millions of eyes, windows to millions of souls, have gazed where I gaze makes this place feel more solid. More real. More electric.

Being dwarfed by the two huge bell towers, I feel that here more than anywhere. I imagine a Medieval congregation filing through the mammoth wooden doors into their cathedral, the place where they communed with their God. Chills run up and down my spine as we go through those very doors.

Margot and Nico go to sit in pews to pray, and Levi stomps off to look at some relics advertised at the front door, so I wander the cathedral on my own. The interior is curious. Dark and quiet, but also bright and loud. Those who want to marvel at the sheer vastness of the place, somehow contained between walls, a floor, and a roof, can walk the nave, look up, and exclaim. Those who want to think, pace, and dream can wander along the outside aisles, past the little chapels and confessionals and statues, and light candles at altars.

I light one candle for Margot and Nico's grandfather. One for the Jewish people he tried so desperately to save. One for Levi. One for me. I give more Euros than I should to the donation tin.

I sit in a pew. Levi sits next to me. Probably only to rest his feet, but it's still nice.

"Do you think the inside is like the Disney movie?" he asks.

"Sort of," I reply.

"What did they get right?" he asks.

"Well . . . it is big."

"No, really, I didn't notice."

I roll my eyes. "You know what I mean. They got the size and proportion of the place right in the movie."

"But they got the environs totally wrong."

"What?"

"The environs," he says, gesturing awkwardly with his hand, like a penguin waving a fin. "They show steps out front of Notre

Dame in the movie. There are no steps in real life. Also there's a big statue of Charlemagne outside. They don't show that."

"I don't know if the Charlemagne statue was there back when the movie takes place," I tell him.

"Even if it wasn't, they should have included it for visual interest."

"We'll have to go look at it again when we go outside."

"Yeah."

Just then, the entire cathedral fills up in the blink of an eye. People sit down in the pew on either side of us, and before we know it, we're part of a massive crowd. A spotlight shines down on a guy standing up at the front altar. Everybody stands.

I've never been a girl who talks to God. Despite the posters in my room of Notre Dame's towers against a stormy sky, despite the way my heart fluttered when a news story came out about hidden murals being revealed during renovations of Westminster Abbey, despite the book on monastery libraries I got for Christmas, my interest is always scholarly, never spiritual.

But the choir begins to sing. Their voices, some ethereal and high, some full-bodied and low enough to buzz in my throat, fill the entire cathedral all the way up to the magnificent ceiling. Every inch of this enormous space is filled by their voices. They sing a heavenly version of "Ave Maria." I close my eyes and let the music fill me up. In rational, cold daylight, I would tell you that Christian mythology is just that: mythology. In the warm, eternal stone embrace of Notre Dame, I start to cry from the sheer beauty.

I open my eyes and look at Levi, to see if he's slumped over and rolling his eyes like usual. But no—his eyes are closed, he sits up straight, his head tilted slightly backward. His lower lip puckers. My heart melts and fills with a golden, glowing feeling. The music is calming him. Does he feel the same as I do right now? Rested, loved, filled up and rejuvenated? If I wasn't in the middle of a church service, I would get out my camera and take a picture of him. This is the most serene he's ever looked.

While I'm staring at him, his head slowly, slowly falls forward. He nods violently, eyes snapping open, then drifting shut. I have to shove my fist into my mouth to stifle a burst of laughter.

He isn't rejuvenated and calmed by the music. He's falling asleep.

I laugh so hard and so silently that even more tears fall down my face and the pressure from keeping in the laughter makes my eyeballs feel like they're going to explode. When the service finally ends and Levi wakes, he's automatically in a horrible, horrible mood. I don't get to wander around the outside of the cathedral, admiring it for as long as I'd like to, but it's okay. It was worth it, seeing Levi at his most vulnerable.

Levi does still want to inspect the Charlemagne statue outside, though. It's made of aged copper, turned blue from oxidization and raised high on a stone platform. Levi walks around it, hands in his pockets, frowning up at it. Margot and Nico are still in the church, so I'm all by myself, watching Levi—until I become aware of a pair of boys a few yards away from me, obviously talking about me.

"Stop it, James," one hisses in a very thick Scottish accent. "Just ask her! Don't take secret pictures like a fucking creep!"

"It's okay, Gable," James says. "It's fine."

I sneak a glance at them. One, a blond in what looks like a private school uniform, has his camera pointed in my general direction, eyes fixed on the display. The other, a tall black boy rocking dreadlocks tied back with a green plaid bandana, paces behind him, looking irritated beyond words. He wears the same school jacket as his friend, but paired with tight jeans that show off powerful-looking thighs, and chunky combat boots.

They both see me looking. Blondie almost drops his camera and Dreadlocked Rocker's eyes go very, very round.

I stare them down. The silence is the most awkward thing I've ever experienced. "Are you taking pictures of me?" I finally ask.

"No," Dreadlocked Rocker says, while the blond boy says, "Yes."

"Well, which is it?"

Dreadlocked Rocker opens his mouth to speak, but Blondie holds up his hand.

"Sorry," he says. "We're taking pictures for a poster for our band, and you looked just about perfect, standing there in this bloody gorgeous sunshine, staring thoughtfully into the distance . . . y'know, very *deep*."

He has a strong British accent that I can't help but smile at.

"He should've asked your permission first," Dreadlocked Rocker says, in that rough, burred Scottish accent. "James is sorry, isn't he?"

He jabs James in the back, and James winces.

"Ouch! Yes, yes, I'm sorry." He sticks out his hand. "I'm James, by the way. My mate here's Gable."

I shake his hand. "I'm Keira."

Gable's eyes are fixed on the ground. When he ventures a glance up at me, I smile at him. His lip hitches upward.

*Gable*. What an adorable name.

"So, err," James says. "Can I take your picture?"

"Um, sure." My hands automatically fly to my tangled hair. "What do you want me to do?"

"Sit there." He points to a nearby bench. "And, like, gaze contemplatively at the cathedral. Or, no, better idea! Lean against that lamp post and gaze contemplatively at the cathedral."

We go with the lamp post. I'm not sure what to do, so I just lean against it, my hand wrapped loosely around the pole, and stand there. James shoots from behind me, and when he shows me his shots a few minutes later, I'm shocked at how awesome they look. Anonymous girl, old iron lamp post, cathedral, all bathed in sun and shadow. I even like the way my hair looks, and the word that comes to mind when I see my arm wrapping around the cast-iron post is *soft*, not *fat* or *flabby*.

"This'll look great," James says. "We could even use this for the album cover, couldn't we, Gable?"

Gable nods before returning his gaze to the ground. He bites his bottom lip. I can't take my eyes off him.

"So, Keira," James says, flashing his pearly whites. "Where you from? The old U. S. of A.?"

"Yeah. Seattle."

That reminds me: Levi. I scan for him and find him still wandering near the Charlemagne statue, a flock of pigeons following him. He squints in my direction, obviously pissed off. Sudden sadness pricks me, seeing him standing alone so far away.

But I don't want to stop talking to James—Gable, even less.

"Seattle, that's so cool," James says. "Kurt Cobain, yeah?"

"Yeah, that's right."

"I'm from Manchester," he says. "Go to school in Edinburgh, though. That's where Gable's from, if you hadn't picked up on his *glorrrrrrious Sco'ish ahccent*."

He elbows Gable, who sways with it. I grin.

"So what are you guys doing in Paris?"

I kind of direct the question to Gable, but James answers again.

"Playing a few shows with our band. That's why we're designing the poster—left it a bit late." He winks. "You should come, Keira. The first show is tomorrow, at this bistro not too far from here. It's going to be sweet."

"Um, yeah, maybe."

Levi is all-out glaring at me now. I reach out my hand and gesture "one minute." He rolls his eyes.

"D'you use TextAnywhere? I can text you all the info."

I give it to him, somewhat hurriedly.

"I really have to go now," I say, pointing at Levi. "My brother's getting impatient."

"We're sorry to keep you," Gable murmurs. He grabs James's arm. "We'll just be on our way now, won't we?"

"Nice to meet you, Miss Keira!" James says, snapping his fingers and pointing them at me. "See you at the show, yeah?"

I nod. "Bye," I say to Gable.

He smiles shyly. "Bye."

I watch them walk away for a few seconds. James jogs to keep up with Gable's long, loping strides. Gable turns and glances back at me. Our eyes lock. I blush.

I return to Levi, who immediately launches into some story about what the pigeons did when he gave them cookie crumbs from his pocket, but I can't concentrate because I'm still stuck on Gable. Oh my God, so cute.

Paris has finally decided to be good to me.

# Chapter Fifteen

The next day, we stroll through the Luxembourg Gardens. It's lovely, of course, but the pamphlet mentioned that the gardens were only opened to the public after the revolution, and of course that got my little communist into a kerfuffle.

"Stupid monarchy," he growls as he walks pigeon-toed along the garden path beside me. "All this was planted and arranged for them and they just kept it away from the People. Like nature isn't for everybody."

"Stop being such a pessimist and enjoy the freaking flowers," I snap, picking up my pace.

Then my phone rings. It's Mom, calling through TextAnywhere. I'm instantly struck by an *uh-oh* feeling. I've texted her a few times and gotten replies, but the times I've called our home phone no one has answered. She was probably just out grocery shopping, but right now she's probably pissed that I haven't stayed up all night trying to call her in the evening in Pacific Time. This should be a fun phone call.

"Keira? Hello?" she says the instant I answer.

"Hi, Mom!"

"How are you guys? Is Levi with you?"

"Of course he is. We're good. Walking in the Luxembourg Gardens."

I wander to a spindly little tree by the side of the path. Levi inspects a flowerbed nearby, frowning at it. I can't hold in my laugh.

"What are you laughing at?" Mom asks tensely.

"Oh, Levi's just glaring at some flowers like they personally insulted him. It's hilarious."

She goes quiet for a second. "How is he? You've barely updated me the whole time you've been there."

"That's because there's been nothing to report, really. Nothing I couldn't text you about. I called the landline a couple times, but you didn't answer."

She pauses for a second. "You know I never answer the land-line. You should have texted in those cases."

She always answers the landline, especially nowadays that it could be a call from Levi's doctors. Is she trying to make *me* feel bad when *she's* the one who didn't answer the phone? What the hell?

"Okay, I'm sorry," I say. "I'll update more, I swear."

Mom sighs. "How's Levi?"

"I already told you, fine. Watching some birds right now."

"I mean behavior-wise."

There's so much I could say. He may have convinced me to have sympathy for Hitler, he ruined the French monarchy for me, and he gave me a heart attack when he disappeared after *Les Mis.* He held it together when I fell apart at the Louvre. Maybe I should tell her about those things, but she'd freak out, especially over the Louvre incident. *You can't even keep yourself together? How can I trust you with Levi? Blah blah blah . . .*

I'm doing perfectly well with him. She'll see when we land back at SeaTac in ten days. We're fine.

"He's good, Mom. Really."

Quiet again. Then: "You aren't leaving him alone, are you?"

"What? Of course not!"

"There are no . . . boys in the picture, are there?"

Huh? Gable's face springs up in my mind and my stomach twists. How could Mom know about him? How could she know I'm planning on going to their show?

"Um . . .?"

"Levi texted and told me you were talking to some boys yesterday," she says carefully.

Oh my fucking God, Levi.

"I just got caught up in a conversation at Notre Dame. Am I not allowed to talk to people here?"

"Not at your brother's expense," she says. "He said you ignored him and talked to them for over an hour."

"That is an actual lie! It was, like, ten minutes, tops." I glare at Levi, who paces the path up ahead. "You know Levi—he has the patience of a gnat."

"I know. Just . . . keep taking care of him, all right?"

*What else would I be doing?* "Yes. Of course."

"I love you," she says, like a peace offering.

"Love you, too," I answer.

Then we hang up, and I watch Levi kick the dirt about fifty feet ahead of me on the path, frowning back at me.

"You coming?" he shouts.

※ ※ ※

I'm annoyed at Levi for telling on me. Annoyed that Mom thinks I would abandon my brother for a couple of boys.

But mostly I'm annoyed with myself, because no matter how much I try to dissuade myself, I keep thinking about Gable.

Half of my brain is like, *finally.* Here's the Parisian romance you always dreamed of. You deserve this! You deserve to go to his show and fall completely, utterly in love with him. You deserve to spend hours talking to him backstage and make all the groupies jealous when he takes your hand. You go, girl!

And the other half is like, you're the stupidest girl in the world. You're so obsessed with this guy you saw for like five minutes that our self-guided walking tour of the *6e arrondissement* doesn't feel real. And you'll probably never see him again, anyway.

Unless Levi lets me go to the show.

"It would be fun," I had told Levi last night. "Live music is always fun."

He made a spectacular show of rolling his eyes. He didn't have to speak for me to know what he meant.

When I was in middle school and mooning over Darren Troy, my grades dropped like rocks because I spent all my time daydreaming and plotting ways to put myself in his path. With Jacques, I was borderline insane. Nothing could pull me away from him. Not even Levi— especially not Levi. Levi was everything I was trying to escape; Jacques was everything I was running toward. Now I know he was just the ugly side of Paris.

Paris isn't always a snooty asshole with a distinguished nose and arching eyebrows. Sometimes, Paris is a tall, shy boy holding back his dreads with a green plaid bandana. That would be worth running toward, right?

And, of course, Paris is pastries and chocolate with Levi and hearing him almost purr in happiness when we turn a corner and come across what looks like a Medieval castle, plunked right in the center of a regular neighborhood. It looks like Hogwarts, right within the Parisian city limits.

"What *is* this place?" Levi asks. His voice actually moves up and down; no monotone.

I look for a sign and find it: *Musée de Cluny.*

"Oh my God," I gasp. "This is the museum with all the Medieval art and tapestries and stuff!"

"Can we go to it?" Levi asks. His fingers clamp onto my sleeve.

We pay for tickets and go inside. The museum is packed full of stone statues with somber, long faces, a million sad King Arthurs.

"Did everyone look the same back in ye olde times?" Levi says with an honest-to-God laugh.

"I just don't think they really had a science for reproducing facial features yet," I say. "They just had Default Old-Timey Face and Generic Martyr Crying Out in Pain Face."

"Hey," Levi says, tugging at my sleeve. "Look at these guys."

There's an exhibit of stone faces, chipped away from their bodies, on pikes. Grotesque, but fascinating.

Levi points at the card identifying them. "This says they used to be on the front of Notre Dame."

My jaw drops. "Holy crap, these are the old apostles!"

I lean in closer to them. These are the faces of the old apostle statues that used to line the façade of Notre Dame, the ones pulled down by revolutionaries because they thought they represented the monarchy. Oh, the things these faces saw—mob mentality and pitchforks and the fires of revolution. I can't take my eyes off them.

Levi tugs my sleeve.

"What?"

He points to a sign that says THE LADY AND THE UNICORN, THIS WAY.

We follow the arrow-shaped signs into a room dominated by a tapestry, rich with deep red and gold. In it, a woman sits in a forest, a unicorn approaching her and letting her pet it.

When I was seven years old, I loved unicorns. I ate, slept, and breathed unicorns. I had this cheap paperback book filled with stories and drawings of different kinds of unicorns from different countries' mythologies, and it grew battered and eventually lost a ton of pages from me leafing through it every day.

One day, Mom took Levi and I to this huge park on the other side of town, one we didn't get to go to that often. There were acres of forest, complete with streams with makeshift log bridges, where we would make forts and have imaginary sword fights. There was a secret pond in the forest, far from the park area where the moms would sit on benches and read Oprah's latest book club pick and talk about mom stuff. The pond had a small island, separated from the mainland by a strip of swamp with a rickety path of stones. While Levi played lightsaber with a stick he found, I picked my way onto the island, because it looked like the perfect place for a unicorn to live.

I knew unicorns only came to virgins, and even if I wasn't sure exactly what that meant, I knew it had something to do with being a young girl, and I definitely was one of those. I stood on the island, which was ringed by trees but clear in the center, and waited. The only sounds were wind in the trees and Levi's distant wooshing lightsaber sound effects. I stood, and I waited. Then I sat and waited for a long time, but I didn't give up. I was sure a snowy white unicorn would appear at any moment.

Of course, no unicorn ever came. I was probably only there about ten minutes before Levi ambled over the stone path and found me, dragging me back into our game. But I've never forgotten those ten, spine-tingling minutes when I was sure a miracle was about to happen.

Looking at the tapestry now, I feel like I've always been that lady in the tapestry. Sitting in a forest, waiting for hours—the only difference is her unicorn actually came. Sure, she was only the lure so the hunters could slay it, but it came nonetheless.

"I can't believe it's so bright," Levi murmurs. "It's impeccably preserved."

He continues chatting happily as we tour the rest of the museum, but I can only listen and think. About how I'm still the girl waiting for the unicorn, and in recent years that unicorn was

Europe. I was the girl waiting for her destiny to come to her, and when she finally arrived there, it's like the hunters seized it.

Nothing about this trip is ideal. Nothing is like I planned.

I wanted a unicorn; I got a shaggy, stubborn donkey.

So I allow myself to cling to the tiny hope of Gable. Maybe he's the missing horn.

# CHAPTER SIXTEEN

We walk home (I can't believe I'm starting to refer to Hoteltastique as home), and as we wander through the Latin quarter, I try to find the exact words to tell Levi about James and Gable's show, but I'm only able to mention it when we get back and the hotel room door closes. Levi immediately grabs the TV remote and crashes down on his bed. I wince and hope the downstairs hotel guests aren't trying to sleep or anything.

I blurt out, "So I'm going to that concert tonight."

Levi says, in his signature monotone, "Why?"

"Just to check it out. See if their music is any good."

"You just want to see that guy."

"No," I lie. "I just want to go and hear them play, all right? No big deal." I hang up my jacket in the closet, facing away from him. It's easier to lie that way.

"You're just going to leave me here alone?"

"You can come if you want," I point out.

He frowns, flipping through channels. "I don't want to."

"Well, then, who's holding who hostage?"

Levi's eyebrows furrow. I search his face to see if he's hurt. What is wrong with me, wanting to see him hurt?

He murmurs, "Nothing good is on in English tonight. And it feels weird when you're not here," he adds.

Tears prickle in my eyes and I wish I could take back any mean thing I ever did to him. What *is* wrong with me? I don't want him to be afraid. I don't want him to *ever* be afraid, or feel anything bad, ever.

Once was enough.

I sit down next to him on the bed and pat his broad, soft back. He leans away from me.

"You're safe," I say, swallowing the lump in my throat. "This place isn't dangerous, Levi."

"I know, but it still feels weird."

"Scary?"

"No." His voice is an aggressive grunt now. "Just weird, okay?"

I nod.

"Promise you'll come home if the music sucks or it's boring," he says.

"I promise," I say. "I won't be gone for too long, Lev. You'll probably fall asleep soon anyway. We had a long day."

He grunts again. I go to the bathroom to shower and get changed.

I didn't bring any pretty clothes with me, only jeans, yoga pants, and plain shirts. A floral print, gauzy blouse is the closest thing I have to something fancy. I pair it with my nicest yoga pants and the effect is sort of romantic and carefree, I guess. The hotel hair dryer is completely useless, though, so the outfit is topped off with my sopping wet hair. I pull on my shoes, grab my travel purse, and head for the door.

"Be good," I tell Levi.

"Hurry up," he says.

Walking out of the hotel room, hearing the door click behind me, feels so wrong. Every step I take down the hall feels wrong. The descending elevator feels like it's stealing me away from where I should be, and as I cross the lobby, I wish the smiling desk attendant would scold me for leaving Levi up there alone.

The metro station is full of dolled-up people with somewhere to go. All of them are prettier than me and have someone to laugh with, but I'm still one of them, and that makes me feel a little better. It's been a long time since I last dressed up and went out. The last time was prom night.

*It's not going to happen this time.* This time is different, I swear.

Everything Levi said amounted to "Don't leave me." He's always convinced abandonment is on the horizon.

I think of our father, who was always shouting at Mom. He didn't like anything much, but he liked Levi. He built the treehouse for him and play-acted military battles across the terrain of our backyard, the general to Levi's plastic army guys. Levi adored him, basking in his love when it was there, left to flounder when it was gone.

Dad moved out when I was eight. Levi was six, and he clung to Dad's leg and cried for him not to go. Dad yelled and shook his leg. He said Levi was too old for that shit. Too old to not want to be walked out on?

There were visits, but they didn't last long, and they became very few and far between. Now there's just silence.

That silence must affect Levi a lot. I've never really thought of that. I've made my peace with the whole situation; I have Josh, who's the best father figure I could ask for. I imagine losing Josh—him walking out, him passing away—and my throat blocks up right here in the metro car. I couldn't handle it. How could I expect Levi to handle that feeling?

Thinking about all this while the metro speeds me in the opposite direction of Levi makes me uncomfortable, but I won't let myself regret leaving. It's just for an hour or two. He's got to learn the difference between leaving for a few hours and leaving forever. I don't have to feel guilty over this. I deserve a few hours by myself, in *Paris*, don't I?

Yes. Yes, I do. I store all the painful thoughts in the back of my mind. I'll deal with them tomorrow.

⌘ ⌘ ⌘

I finally find the bistro where The Elegant Noise is playing. It's less than packed, but still with a substantial amount of diners—they're drinking more than they're eating. It's dark and moody. I can't see any faces, except by the light of the candles on each table.

Other girls cling to friends if they haven't got a guy on their arm, and I'm feeling disastrously alone. I move through the crowd toward the bar. I need a glass of something in my hand to ward away the nerves, even if I'm only going to sip it—getting drunk or even tipsy in a foreign country when I'm technically by myself sounds like a bad idea.

I don't see any sign of a stage until I have my glass of cheap wine and I weave my way through the tables of the L-shaped room. The short branch of the L opens to a patio strung with white Christmas lights, cozy but bright. I pick a table out there, near a makeshift stage, where a boy in a kilt sets up a drum kit.

The drummer sits down, tapping experimentally as the crowd claps and hollers half-heartedly. James comes out from the bistro, cherry wood guitar slung over his back, and he whips it around to his front, grinning and winking.

Gable slinks out, bass at the ready, head down. He crouches to plug it into an amp and adjust some dials. James steps up to the microphone.

"Good evening, Paris," he says. "We are The Elegant Noise, and you sure are looking lovely tonight."

A crowd has somehow conjured itself into existence, blocking my view. I stand, but I still can't see. As The Elegant Noise begin to play, I place one foot on my chair, the next on my table, and perch on the concrete patio wall. The perfect view, as long as I don't get yelled at by the manager.

The music sounds pretty good—rock with a slow tempo, James whining lyrics I can't really make out—but I'm not really listening. My eyes drink up every inch of Gable. His bass is deep, dark purple, and he plucks the strings with expert speed. A speaker near my head pumps the agile, walking bass lines into me as I watch his fingers travel up, down, and across the neck of his instrument.

He's in a black button-down shirt with a black tie under a black vest. Monochromatic black against his dark skin and hair just pulls at something inside me. He looks like an old-world jazz player with new world twists, like the same green plaid bandana that ties his hair back. I have a feeling this is his signature thing.

I don't know how long the show lasts. They play an indeterminate number of songs, most of them sounding exactly the same as the ones before, James flirting with the crowd in between, and then it's over. The band disappears inside the bistro. It's late, and the crowd wants to hardcore party now.

What am I supposed to do now? Go home? Try to find James and Gable? That's what I want to do, but I don't want to be *that* girl.

I go to the ladies' room, since that's as good a place as any to start, and when I exit, I find James outside the door engaged in a very enthusiastic conversation with a tattooed, pierced girl. Gable stands off to the side, one hand locked awkwardly around the other elbow, one foot tapping a frenzied rhythm.

James suddenly grabs my arm as I walk by. The girl he's talking to glares daggers at me.

"Hey, nice to see you! How'd you like the show?"

"It was good," I tell him and give a lame thumbs-up.

James goes back to the other girl and my eyes fall on Gable. Summoning all my courage, I walk around James and Punk Girl to Gable's other side. I try to smile, but I think my face just spasms. "Hi," I say.

Gable's face spasms in almost the exact same way. "Hey."

He wears black Converse sneakers—cool—and there's a yellow design on them I can't quite make out. I point. "What's the yellow?"

He lifts up his trouser leg. The sides of the sneakers are splashed with a sketchy Batman logo.

"That's so awesome," I splutter.

He smiles properly this time. "Thanks." He says something else, but the music playing is too loud for me to hear.

"Sorry?" I say, leaning in.

He repeats himself but I don't catch it, again. Crap, he's going to think I'm a moron. I shake my head and lift my hands in an I'm-sorry-I-can't-hear-jack-shit kind of way. He motions for me to follow him.

The bistro has gotten way more crowded; we have to push and thread our way out. It's like winding through a corn maze, if the corn was people and you could easily see the other side of the maze, but the corn is too drunk to let you through.

We finally stumble out the doors and Gable pulls me aside. It's raining, droplets so fine it's just mist.

"I'm sorry, *what* were you saying in there?" I blurt out.

He laughs and reaches up to adjust his hair under the bandana.

"I was saying 'do you want to go outside?' but we've since done that."

I grin, crossing my arms over my chest. I wish I had another drink, or just something to do with my hands instead of looking like a total spaz.

"This is much better," I tell him. "I'm not really a fan of crowded, loud places."

"Me either," he says. "Can't hear a bleedin' word coming out of anyone's mouth."

*His accent.* I have to rein in my smile, dial it back to normal. I don't want to be one of those American girls who probably go nuts over his accent every day.

"That's ironic," I say. "Considering you probably play in these types of places all the time."

Gable shrugs. "That's just playing bass. Don't need to hear anything else while I play, just the drums. And hearing drums is no problem, ever, really." He laughs. "Um . . . did you like the show?"

"Yeah, you guys were good."

"It wasn't our best night," he confesses. "I fucked up a couple o'times. James's playing was sort of a mess—he always concentrates too much on his singing. We're usually better. Not a lot better, but . . . a little."

"Maybe I'm just not that hard to impress," I say, and we both laugh.

"Sorry, I just realized I've forgotten your name," Gable says, wincing. "Mine's Gable, Gable McKendrick."

"Keira Braidwood."

"Keira," he repeats. "And you were from Seattle?"

He pronounces the T's in Seattle and I love it.

"Actually, I'm from Shoreline, a few miles outside of Seattle."

"Close enough," he says. "I'm actually from Leith, but I always round up to Edinburgh. Otherwise no one'd have any idea."

"Right, exactly."

And with that, we have nothing left to say. I giggle and rub the back of my neck. He laughs, looking down at his feet. His teeth slip out of his previously closed-lipped smile. They're completely straight and sparkling white.

The words just pop out: "You have *amazing* teeth."

His smile slips. His teeth disappear behind his soft-looking, pillowy lips.

"Um, thanks," he says. "I wonder where James has got to."

"He was talking to that girl . . ."

"God, then he could be anywhere." Gable smiles a little again, lips closed. "Could be halfway to Monaco by now if she so much as mentioned it."

I laugh. "Bit of a womanizer?"

"He'll do *anything* for any member of the female species—and I do mean species. He's a slave to his golden retriever, Betsy."

I laugh in a quick burst, far louder than I intended. Gable grins and leans backward, trying to peer inside the club past the bouncer and through the door.

"I don't see him," he says with a sigh. "I'll try texting him." He gets out a slick phone and types quickly. After a minute or two, he looks up. "He says to, and I quote, make his apologies to Miss Keira, for he will not be at leisure to join us any time soon." Gable sighs again, putting his phone away. "And that's the end of it."

"Is he always like this?" I ask Gable.

Gable nods. "Long as I've known him."

"How close are you guys?"

"Honestly, not all that close. We're roommates, and we play music together, but that's pretty much it. Girls are his life, school is mine."

He doesn't elaborate, so I ask: "What are you studying? Are you in college, or . . .?"

"University," he corrects, winking. "You Americans and your 'college.'"

Oh God, I'm a moron.

We sink into silence. He kicks his Batman sneakers against the pavement. Without James being all exuberant and talkative, I feel like there's nothing stringing us together. My heart is in my throat. He's just so pretty! I can't stop looking at his lips and wondering if they're as soft as they look. His eyes dart around. I'm losing him.

I say, as brightly as possible, "What shall we do? Or, do you have to go, or . . ."

"No, I don't have to go," he says. "I mean, not if you don't want me to."

"I don't want you to." The tips of my ears burn.

"Okay." He smiles, closed-lipped. "What shall we do?"

"I have no idea," I confess. "What does one do at . . ." I get out my phone and check the time. "Eleven at night in Paris?"

He says, "One finds a good late-night eatery and puts something in one's belly, and then one goes for a walk in the rain and just enjoys the company of pretty American girls."

Reining in my smile isn't an option anymore.

"Do you have much experience in the field of enjoying the company of pretty American girls?" I ask. Look at me, I'm flirting!

He winks—*he actually winks*. "That bit is a first for me."

⚜ ⚜

Gable has never had a Nutella crêpe.

"How could you?" I demand. "How could you allow yourself to be in Paris without eating a Nutella crêpe? Do you not understand what that is? Nutella? Crêpe? Put together?"

"I know," he says, studying the menu at the crêpe place we found. "I'm just always in the mood for savory. Ham and cheese and steak and the like. Can't resist that."

"I'm always in the mood for dessert ones. Even at dinner time."

"Dessert for dinner?" He looks at me with one eyebrow raised. "You're a loon."

"You never have dessert for dinner, are you serious? How about breakfast for dinner?"

He shakes his head in mock seriousness. "The American public education system is even worse than I thought."

Gable gets honey ham and capicolli, with Swiss cheese and a ton of herbs, and I get my signature Nutella. I spring for bananas, too. We sit at a tiny table in the tiny shop—has there ever been a crêpe shop in all the history of crêpe shops that is bigger than a jumbo-sized matchbox?—and unwrap our plastic cutlery. I eye his crêpe and I see him eyeing mine.

"Why don't we just share?" I ask. "You know you want it. I want it, too."

"Oh, do you?" he asks, laughing. "Well, then . . ."

He reaches over with his fork and steals the square of crêpe I just cut for myself.

"Well, then, I'm going to steal this rather juicy-looking shred of ham. And this crispy part."

"Be my guest, madam. My life is but to serve you."

I laugh, because it's a joke, but part of me is being stupid. Part of me is hoping his jokes expose rather than mask. Maybe he's feeling the same fluttery happiness I am? Just maybe, for the first time, could a cute boy dig me as much as I dig him?

My inner realist tells me to lower my expectations. Gable is just really charming and funny and he's not trying to be charming or funny *at* me. I need to live in the moment for once, not constantly nurse my high hopes.

"This is really good," he says after his first bite of Nutella-banana deliciousness. His hand brushes mine as he steals another piece.

I swallow hard. How could that have been accidental?

Stop it. Stop using everything as a measuring stick for how much he does or doesn't like you.

"Snack tax," I say, stealing another bite of his crêpe.

He laughs. "Snack tax?"

"That's what my mom says, whenever she steals a bite of mine or my brother's treats."

"That's brilliant. My mom would just use guilt, with no regard for the deep psychological scars it would leave behind."

"Mothers, right?"

He nods, going back to devouring his crêpe.

I want to ask questions: Does your mom go crazy when you're abroad, too? What's Edinburgh like? Do you have a girl-friend or any kind of attachment, however slight, back home? But my inner realist, again, tells me not to. Too much, too soon, with someone you probably won't ever see again. Skip all the get-ting-to-know-you stuff and just have fun. Besides, asking about someone's mother when you've known them for just a few hours is nosy and weird.

I play it safe: "So what are you studying?"

He shrugs. "Just taking random classes right now. 'Exploring my options,' as the academic counsellors like to call it. Which is all right, if it wasn't the state I've been in for two years now."

If he's been in college—university—for two years, that could make him . . . nineteen? Twenty?

"I just can't really seem to settle into any particular disci-pline. Everything interests me, and nothing interests me. You know? I like too many different areas for there to be one feasi-ble future career that incorporates everything, and if I settled too far into one interest, the other parts of my brain would feel unstimulated."

"I think I know what you mean," I say. "Sometimes I wish I could live ten or twenty lives with all the things I want to pursue."

"What do you want to pursue?" he asks.

"French. Second to that would be German, and after that, I guess architecture, mostly Gothic, but I also, like, *love* Baroque and Rococo. I'd love to do something like art conservation, maybe. Unless I go for accounting or law instead, which I might. More money there."

Gable smiles, without his perfect teeth. "Sounds like you're all set," he says. "I'm sure you'll be successful, no matter what you choose."

"I'm not so sure," I say, sighing. "Anyway, what are your interests, if they're so irreconcilable?"

"Physics was my best subject, as well as music. I played bass all through school. I'm really interested in the mining industry, since Pa's worked the mines all his life. I also love drawing and painting, I dunno, I can't really explain that one."

"You don't have to *explain*. I can't explain why I'm so obsessed with languages I can barely speak."

I say that, but I think of all the times I've used my French on this trip and I swell a little with pride. I've managed to get by—more than get by, actually. All those classes, Rosetta Stone sessions, and language apps on my phone, not to mention all the time and effort I dedicated to them, actually paid off.

"You want to learn," Gable says. "To understand. To make more connections. To give yourself the tools to see more of the world and understand your place in it. Maybe create yourself a whole new place in it. Sound about right?"

"Yeah, I suppose that's it." I stare down at my plate. My chest is full of warmth. He gets it when I didn't even get it.

We finish our crêpes in silence. I can't tell if it's awkward or not, full of rejection or not. Maybe I was prying. I'm so socially inept that I can't tell if asking about someone's deep, abiding passions on a first meeting is okay.

Gable looks up from his plate at me and smiles tentatively. I smile back.

"So?" he asks.

I check my watch again. It's just after midnight. "It's getting pretty late," I admit.

He glances at his phone. "God, you're right. I don't even know where you're staying or who you're traveling with and if they're expecting you back."

"No, no, it's okay," I say, standing up. He follows suit. "It's just me and my brother, no parents or anything. I should get home to him, though."

"Where are you staying?"

"*Treizième arrondissement*," I say, just a tiny bit embarrassed.

Gable's eyes widen. "That's pretty far! Come on, I'll walk you to the metro. Will you need help finding your way along the routes?"

"No, I'm a metro expert."

"Of course." We exit the crêpe shop and take a couple steps down the road before Gable asks, "How long have you been in town?"

"Almost a week now." It feels both longer and shorter than that simultaneously.

"Short amount of time to become an expert. This can't be your first time in Paris."

"It is. When you want to learn, you learn quickly."

He laughs softly, and we're silent the rest of the walk. It's still drizzling and everybody acts like they've never seen rain before. Lots of umbrellas, even in fine mist, and newspapers or magazines clutched over heads. High heels tap furiously as women dash from doorway to doorway. I'm a Northwest girl; this is nothing.

"Has Paris never had rain before?" I ask as a woman dashes past us, squealing.

"Seattle's pretty rainy, isn't it?" Gable asks.

"It's pretty much the defining characteristic of the area," I say. "Stephenie Meyer owes her fortune to Pacific Northwest weather."

"What?"

"Oh, you know, the author of *Twilight*? The gloomy weather is the trademark of the series."

I look up to see Gable side-eyeing me.

"You aren't a *Twilight* fan, are you?"

"No, no!" I laugh. "Just someone who lives in Washington. You can't escape it. It's become an industry."

"Really?"

"I have cousins in Forks who work as *Twilight* tour guides in the summer. No joke."

Gable gives a low whistle. "Like Harry Potter. Castles in Scotland have gotten a boost in visitors from having Hogwarts appeal."

"I know which series I'd rather live in," I say.

"Definitely. Vampires are so much hotter than wizards."

"No way! Harry Potter wins. Obviously."

"I bet you're a fan of those shirtless werewolves."

"Do you want to see my Ravenclaw crest necklace as proof?" I offer. "It's back in my suitcase, I can show you."

And then I press my hand over my mouth to stifle anything else that could be considered a veiled invitation to come up to my hotel room. Luckily we've reached the metro. We descend the stairs and show our passes and then the hallway parts. I have to go east, he has to go west.

"Well, Keira . . ."

"Yes, Mr. McKendrick?"

He stands, feet apart, hands in his jacket pockets, and makes a face at me. I stick out my tongue. He reaches out his finger like he's going to poke it and pokes my nose instead at the last second. I let out an honest-to-goodness giggle.

"I want to see you again," he says simply.

"I want to see you again, too."

"Tomorrow?"

"Yes."

We exchange TextAnywhere usernames.

"All set?" he says. "I will text you tomorrow and we'll figure something out."

"Okay."

"Okay."

We just stand there, smiling at each other, not making any step toward the hallways we should be walking down right about now. I have to go; he has to go. But neither of us moves.

"Well . . ." He holds his arms out awkwardly. "Hug, I guess?"

I laugh and step into his embrace. My head barely reaches his shoulder. It's sexy.

"See you tomorrow," he says.

I wave and step down the east-bound tunnel. He goes west and out of sight.

I feel like I'm walking on clouds all the way back to the *13e arrondissement*. When I get home, Levi is still up watching TV. The room smells kind of rancid, like body odor and old socks.

"Hey," I say, throwing my purse and jacket over a chair on my way to open the window.

"You took fucking forever."

"Well, I watched the band play for like an hour, then I had dinner and went for a walk with Gable, not to mention the metro ride there and back."

He glares. "Who's Gable? The hipster who doesn't shut up?"

"No, the shy guy."

"The black guy?"

"Yeah."

"Huh." Levi turns back to the TV, which is playing some kind of police detective show in French. "Never thought black guys would be your type."

I don't even know what to say. "Um, what the fuck, Levi?"

"What?" he asks. "That's not racist."

"Yeah, it kind of is."

"I'm just saying, you usually like guys who are all skinny and French. Not black."

I splutter, "I . . . I can't believe I have to tell you not to say things like that, Levi."

"Why not? It's true."

I ignore him, go into the bathroom, and shut the door. I splash water on my face and stand there at the sink, letting it drip down, for a long time. The way he talks like that—it's so . . . inconsiderate. Brash. Naive.

And that's exactly what Levi is. Sheltered. Eccentric. Definitely naive.

His pill bottles line the shelf, staring me down oh-so-innocently. For the millionth time, I wonder what they really do to him. I squeeze my eyes shut and imagine him as a child, running through the years up to today. He shifted over the years. Once he was happy, hyper, giddy. Then he was snappish, moody, offensive, like he is now. I remember the anger he was prone to, and the weeks when silence would emanate from the basement. Which Levi is a product of the pills? Where does he end and the medication begin? Do they take him from zombie to the crackling, sardonic, animated Levi, or vice versa?

*What's real?* I ask the pills. They don't answer.

I'm so confused.

I find his pill tray upside down on the floor by the toilet. I pick it up and set it next to the bottles.

"I just found your pill thing on the floor," I tell him when I've finished changing into my pajamas and brushing my teeth. "Please take better care of your shit."

Levi grunts. He turns the TV off and fiddles with his alarm clock. I drop into bed, not bothering to ask him when he's setting it. I'll wake up whenever I feel like it.

⚬⚬⚬

The alarm goes off at seven. Jerk.

I wait for Levi to turn it off, but he doesn't budge. He's curled into a ball, snoring away. I get up and turn it off.

I wait a little longer, but he doesn't rise, not even when the sun fills the whole room with light. The bakery is open now. I need a croissant. I'm like a robotic homing device, so bent on bread that I almost get run over in the street by a bicycle. Doesn't matter. The only things that matter are warm and delicious and buttery.

When I walk in the door, Margot is busy arranging a tray of croissants under the glass counter. She grins when she sees me.

"*Bon matin*," she says. "*Des croissants?*"

I love that she knows me so well already. "Yes, please!"

She gives me two of the hottest, freshest chocolate croissants, a bonus jam cookie, and tells me to sit while she makes me a "café mocha masterpiece." Her words, not mine. I sit at the table and take out my phone. TextAnywhere shows that I have a message.

*Good morning, miss*, Gable texted. *Hope you slept well.*

I instantly grin.

*I did, thank you sir :)*

"Levi is still in bed?" Margot asks. "Shall I package him some treats for you to take?"

"Yes, please."

*What shall we do today?* Gable texts when I check my phone in the elevator, a paper bag of treats for Levi in my arms.

*I have no idea*, I answer.

*Have you been underground yet?* he asks.

*What?*

*Okay, then I know what we'll do.*

Sounds a little ominous. Underground? I think I might've heard something about Paris having some kind of underground tunnel system or something, but I can't really remember. I knock on our hotel room door, but Levi doesn't answer.

"It's me," I call, knocking again. "My arms are full, open up."

Nothing.

I have to put down the bag of pastries, fumbling for my room key, and open it myself.

"Jeez, lazybones, couldn't even . . ."

Levi is still asleep. It's eight in the morning. This is weird. Sleep deprived or not, he's almost always up at this hour, but here he is, snoring away. I set the paper bag next to him on the bedside table and try to shake him awake, but it doesn't work. He just rolls over and curls into a protective ball. I'm pretty sure he was a hedgehog in a past life. I sigh out loud, trying to sound extra exasperated. Maybe that'll spur him into action, in case he's faking and he really can hear me. But still nothing.

I turn on the TV and sit there, only half-watching. The volume is up loud, but it's not waking him, either. I watch one morning talk show, then the news, and it's getting close to eleven o'clock when I text Gable.

*My brother's refusing to wake up.*

*Does he have to come?* he asks.

Well, no. And he probably wouldn't even want to, and if he did he'd be miserable the whole time.

*We can go without him and you can be back in time to have lunch with him or something,* Gable texts.

Relief floods me. Yes, that sounds perfect. Go out for a little bit, come back in time for lunch. I grab the hotel notepad and pen off the desk and scrawl a note to Levi: *Went out for a bit, back around 2—Keira*

*Okay, let's go,* I text to Gable. *Where shall I meet you?*

Gable texts, *Take the metro to Place Denfer-Rochereau.*

# Chapter Seventeen

Place Denfer sounds identical to *Place d'Enfer*, Place of Hell. On the metro ride, I Google it and find out that it used to actually be called something like Barrier of Hell and Victor Hugo once wrote about it. They renamed it after a war general whose last name happened to be Denfer-Rochereau. Convenient.

The French sure know how to make something spectacular out of an intersection. In the Place Denfer-Rochereau, I count eight (I think) separate roads all coming together at odd angles, creating a shape like an asterisk. Triangular buildings all point to the heart of the star, where a statue of a lion presides. Little, leafy parks occupy the triangular space between the streets, giving the whole place a feel of frantic urban busyness, but also of leisurely walks through a zoo.

Gable waits for me, leaning against the wrought-iron fence outside the metro station. He smiles, no teeth, when he sees me.

"Good morning," I say.

"Aye, 'tis," he says, and I laugh before I have time to wonder whether it's a joke or just the way he talks. He's still smiling, so I figure I had permission to laugh.

"Where exactly are we going?" I ask as he starts to lead me down the street.

"Underground," he says. "The Paris Catacombs."

"Catacombs," I repeat slowly. "What's down there?"

"I can't tell you. It would ruin it."

He leads me to a blackened wood shack with the words Musée des Catacombes de Paris on a sign above the door. The line is short, which doesn't give me much time to prepare myself.

I am going underground.

Inside, after Gable pays for both of our tickets, we are shown to a stone entryway over seemingly endless uneven stone steps that lead down, down, down. An inscription, carved into the stone, reads Arrête! C'est ici l'empire de la mort.

*Stop! This is the empire of death.*

My whole body takes up a new hobby: trembling uncontrollably.

Gable hops down a couple of the steps like it's no big deal. I'm stuck at the top.

"Come on," he says. "Something the matter?" He smiles.

I take a deep breath and take the first step. And then the next. And it gets a bit easier when I'm next to him.

I'm starting to feel okay with this whole descending-into-the-dark-unknown thing as we continue. We aren't alone; there are plenty of tourists ahead and behind us. If everyone else can do this, I can do this. Right?

We reach the bottom of the stairs, and I'm not so sure anymore. The lighting is almost nonexistent, but further ahead of us, it illuminates intricately textured walls with a pattern I can't make out yet. Rough stone? It feels old down here, very old. It *smells* old.

We take a few more steps and it becomes horrifyingly obvious what the lights illuminate. What the walls are made out of.

Bones.

Stacks upon stacks of bones.

Piles of tibias and fibias, their knobby ends facing out, so many I couldn't begin to count them. Layers of them, meters thick, cut with layers, stacks, of skulls.

I clutch Gable's hand and squeeze tight.

"Ouch, Keira," he says, trying to loosen my grip.

I close my eyes against the horrors of the bones. So unapologetic. So undisguised. We are in a room made of the remains of other humans and no one else seems to be petrified by this.

"What is this place?" I whisper.

"An ossuary," he says. "Seriously, Keira, stop squeezing my hand so tight."

Ossuary: a place where they keep bones. I know this word, but I always figured they would be more like offices. Remains filed away in drawers or bags, out of sight. I never, in my wildest nightmares, thought it would mean haphazard stacks, skulls turned outwards to stare at you. Who would do this to other humans? My stomach is a knot of organs, solid as stone.

"The remains of almost six million people lie in the Paris Catacombs," a matter-of-fact tour guide says nearby.

She goes on to name the battles and events where most of the dead came from, and I want to clap my hands over my ears. It's so horrible, the thought of people raiding the battlefield for bodies, collecting all their bones, and piling them down here. Is that how it happened? Or were the people originally in some mass grave, so jumbled together that after decomposition it was impossible to distinguish one from another, and so the ossuary is actually more respectful? I don't know what to think, what to feel.

I let go of Gable's hand when he tries to lead me into yet another bone-lined room.

"I can't," I whisper. "I just can't be down here right now."

I can't see his face very well in the dark; I can't tell what kind of look he's giving me. "Why not?"

"I—I . . ." My palms break out in a sweat. "I just can't, okay?"

Everything is tight. My stomach. My ribcage. My clothes feel like they're suffocating me.

"Okay," Gable says, slowly stepping toward me. "Okay, let's leave, then."

We walk back through the rooms, against the grain of people. We push through tourists on the stairs. Everyone stares.

"Oh, she looks white as a sheet, she does," an old British lady says as I pass her.

"The poor dear," her friend says.

"Little girl scared?" a man cackles. "Scared of a bunch o' bones?"

I hurry my pace and glance up at Gable. I don't really want him to come to my rescue and I don't expect it, but some defense, any defense, would be better than the stillness of his face right now. He's silent and unexpressive as we burst back into the light of the Place Denfer-Rochereau.

My trembling doesn't stop and my heart rate doesn't slow. Gable wants to keep walking, but when I see a bench on the edge of one of the little parks, I sit down. I try to force my tense muscles to relax, but the tightness won't go away.

At first Gable just hovers beside me. When I lean forward to rest my forehead in my hands, he finally sits, but still says nothing.

The Louvre, now the Catacombs . . . what's happening to me?

Finally, my heart rate starts to slow and breathing comes a little easier. "I'm sorry," I say. I force a quick laugh. "I—I've had this thing about death recently. I can't really explain it. Well, actually, I can. I guess I just don't want to feel like even more of an idiot right now."

"You aren't an idiot," he murmurs.

"Who gets scared of a bunch of bones? They obviously can't hurt me."

"Who cares what that guy said." Gable sighs. "I'm sorry. I shouldn't have taken you there."

"You didn't know. Ordinarily, I'd have found it really fascinating, I'm sure. It's just . . . I've had a rough year."

He kicks at a rock. "You can tell me about it, if you want."

"My brother . . . is just really screwed up. We're just finding out he's autistic, and he might have other diagnoses, too. He . . . tried to kill himself a little while ago. So I guess the thought of death is just really not helpful right now."

He winces. "Oh my God, I'm so sorry I took you down there. That was so dumb of me."

"You didn't know."

"I still feel like an idiot."

I smile. "That makes two of us."

He taps his mouth and looks around us, brow furrowed like he's looking for something. I watch his finger tap, tap, tap against his perfect, pillowy bottom lip.

"There are other places you can go underground," he says. "It's technically illegal, and sometimes people do weird shit down there, but there are no body parts."

"No body parts is good. Where are these places?"

"I don't know." He takes out his cell phone. "But I will find out."

⁕⁎⁕

A stop at a hardware store for some supplies and a metro ride later, Gable and I walk into a dark courtyard behind an apartment building in Montparnasse. Dumpsters line one wall, and it looks like that's all this space is used for.

He points across the courtyard. "There's the access."

It's just a manhole.

"Are you sure?"

He nods. "The website says you lift the lid and climb down the ladder."

"Okay," I say, throwing caution to the wind. "Let's do this."

Lifting the manhole lid is the easy part. What's really scary is the ladder down into the earth. Light from the sky illuminates a few rungs, but they descend into complete darkness.

Gable gets out the flashlight we bought and sticks it in his front shirt pocket.

"Here goes nothing," he says, setting his foot on the first step. He looks hopelessly awkward at first, climbing down the first couple rungs with his chest on the ground, but once he's oriented, he looks up at me. "Come on. Easy as pie."

He smiles, and I shake myself before following him. My whole body starts trembling again as I slither down the hole and start the endless descent. The light only lasts a few feet, and then we're in darkness.

"At least I couldn't look down if I wanted to," I say, my voice a desperate laugh.

"You're fine," Gable says. "We're both fine."

I don't know how long we climb, but it starts to feel like forever. My muscles grow sore and my legs start shaking from the effort, not from fear. That's a good sign, I guess.

Gable finally says, "Okay, I'm at the bottom now."

A moment later, my foot touches rocky ground. Gable clicks on his flashlight.

It's more like a room than a cave, with proper square walls and everything, surprisingly large. There's graffiti everywhere, modern tags and older-looking scrawls and drawings. Stubs of candles sit on every flat surface and in every alcove.

"Should we light some of the candles?" Gables asks, pulling out the matchbox we brought. "Or explore a little more with the flashlight?"

The flashlight makes me feel like monsters are lurking in the darkness beyond the beam, and that something is about to jump out at us at any moment, horror movie style. But I sort of want to explore.

"Let's go that way." I point toward a big, arching doorway.

Through the doorway is another, bigger room, with what looks like a low bench running the length of it, candles placed every foot or so. The middle of the room has more makeshift stone benches filling up the center, like church pews.

"I read an article in *National Geographic* about the police finding an illegal movie theatre set up down here," Gable says. "Screen, projector, seats, speakers, everything. Even a bar."

"That's insane," I murmur, speaking quietly so my voice won't echo. "How did they get it all down here?"

"Through the access points, must've been," he says. "There aren't many. You can apparently explore for hours and hours without coming across another access that isn't the one you came in."

I shiver. "Let's stay close to ours."

"Of course. The people who do the hardcore explorations are professionals."

"We are definitely amateur hour," I confirm.

"Strictly."

"Let's light the candles."

Gable takes out the box and offers it to me.

Lighting the candles, of which there seem to be hundreds, illuminates beauty I never thought could be found hundreds of feet below street level. The walls aren't just graffitied; they're covered in murals. There are anonymous faces, painted with the care of any artist working on canvas. There's a seaside landscape, so detailed you can make out the wings of seagulls in the distance and expressions on the faces of beachgoers. There are plenty of naked bodies, writhing and dancing and performing acts not safe for the eyes of children. I find myself blushing as we light candles and uncover more images in the dark.

When the whole room is blazing with soft light, we sit down on one of the benches. The most spectacular, expansive painting of all is splayed across one wall.

It's Notre Dame, brought to life ten feet high, each detail so crisp and precise I feel like I'm once again standing in the square, looking up at the towers. The bluebird sky, the trees, and the Seine are all faithfully rendered, and some shadowy human figures populate the walkways. A few are up in the towers, looking down.

*From whence came the stones*, the artist has written below their amazing painting.

"These caves used to be mines and quarries," Gable says. "This must be where they quarried the stone for Notre Dame."

"It's beautiful," I whisper. "What kind of person paints something like this so far away from human eyes? Almost no one is going to see it."

"They wanted the right people to see it," he whispers back.

Gable's breath tickles my neck. It makes me shiver again. I turn my head toward him and he kisses me. I stiffen. His lips push gently, like they're asking a question, and slowly, I melt. His hands slide around my waist.

My whole body is like, *oh, so this is kissing*.

I quickly find that good kissing puts me in a trance. The only thing I care about is being as close as possible. When my arms can't hold him tight enough, I find myself scrambling into his lap just to get closer. For a second, I despair when he breaks free, but my whole body bursts into happy shivers when I find he only broke the kiss to cover my neck and shoulders in matching kisses. I realize I'm being weirdly quiet so I make a noise to let him know how happy I am and then it echoes in the cave and scares me.

Gable plants one last, slow, lingering kiss on my lips and sits back. His eyes are half-closed, dreamy, as they take in my face. I must look shocked and wired. That's how I feel.

"Hi," he whispers.

"Oh, hello," I whisper back.

"How are you?"

"Good. You?"

"Never better."

I grin and a giggle escapes, echoing. Gable laughs and clamps his lips shut afterward.

"Don't," I say, touching him. "Just let yourself smile."

He won't stop biting his lips. I try to force his jaws apart and he starts laughing, exposing his beautiful ivory teeth.

"Why do you hide them?" I ask.

"My teeth?" he asks. "Because most of 'em aren't real."

"What?"

"They're implants," he says. "I lost most of my teeth when I was younger. Couldn't afford a dentist, they . . . well, they jumped ship. I had to get a ton pulled. So yeah. When you spend most of your life having people stare at you for it, you tend not to like smiling."

I murmur, "That sounds horrible. I'm sorry."

He shrugs.

"But they're beautiful. I would never guess they aren't real. I would just think you had amazing brushing and flossing skills."

He laughs and I'm so close to him it makes me bounce. "Then I'm ashamed of them for making me a liar."

"I don't think you're a liar. Unless you're lying about *this*, right now."

"What's this?"

I gesture between the both of us. I'm still sitting in his lap, facing him, my legs clamped tight on either side of him, his arms wrapped around me, supporting me. I imply the kiss, everything.

"I would never jerk you around on purpose."

"But you might do it accidentally?" I joke.

"Well . . . I kind of forget where the ladder we came down is," he admits.

We both laugh, frantically, and then quickly sober up.

"I really, really would rather not get lost down here," I say. "What if we get attacked by cave dwellers? What if there are monsters down here? What if we slowly starve to death?"

"Calm down," he says with another laugh. "The worst things down here are the piles of bones."

I think he quickly realizes that was a horrible thing to say.

"Oh God. I'm sorry. Please don't let your eyeballs pop out."

"I'm okay," I say, "as long as we get the hell out of here like, *yesterday*."

"And we will, I promise," Gable says. "Now why don't we start with you getting off me?"

I climb awkwardly out of his lap and stand, brushing imaginary dust or lint or something off my pants. Must pretend this is no big deal, must pretend this is no big deal . . .

"Should we douse the candles?" he asks. "Or leave them going? I don't think there's much of a fire hazard down here."

"If the candles all burn down, the next explorers won't have any light."

"I guess you're right. Well, start blowing."

He turns the flashlight on and I blow on each candle to extinguish it. Gable gets a little show off-y, trying his hand at pinching the still-burning wicks.

"Doesn't hurt too bad," he says.

"Stop it!" I resist the urge to slap his hand away as he does it again. "Stop it, you'll hurt yourself."

"Won't."

"Do it on your own time," I tease. "I don't feel like hanging out in a French hospital. Now get out of my way, I'm blowing."

"You certainly are," he says, muffling a laugh.

"Ew!"

It's a good thing we're joking and keeping things light, because the darkness is starting to stifle me. With every candle we blow out, we re-mask more artwork. I leave Notre Dame for last, because it's the last we discovered and the last I want to lose. Finally we're in a dark room, with no sign of the beauty to be had. Only blackness.

Gable reaches for my hand and leads me back to the first room and to the ladder.

"You found it pretty fast," I remark.

"I told you I wouldn't let you get lost," he says. "You climb up first. I'll keep the monsters at bay behind you."

I roll my eyes before I start to climb, but when he can't see me, I unleash my grin. I've never had anyone want to battle the monsters back for me. I've always been the protector, never the protected.

Everything is going swimmingly until my legs turn to jelly halfway up the ladder. Pain shoots through my thighs to my shaking knees. My hands grip the rung so tight I'm terrified my knuckles will shatter and I'll fall, despite my every effort to cling to life. Inevitable. Good-bye.

*Levi.*

"You can do it," Gable says, voice light and full of goddamn optimism. "One step at a time, you can do it."

I shake my head. He can't see it in the dark—of course he can't—but now my voice won't work. I squeeze my eyes shut against the tears, but it doesn't matter. It's dark, dark, dark all around me.

"Keira?" He touches my calf, so gently. "Up and out, okay?"

"I can't."

"You can. You have to."

My arms tremble now. The only things keeping me on this ladder, and they're going to fail me. My teeth chatter. It's so cold.

There's a click from below me. I glance down. Gable, one arm holding him to the ladder, has maneuvered the flashlight out of his pocket. It illuminates the rusty, dirty, wet walls around us. We're in a *tiny tube* barely wider than our bodies. The dark beneath Gable is chasing us. It's so, so dark. I loop my arm around the ladder, let it support my body. My muscles unclench a little. I can stay like this, can't I?

Light floods down from a tiny circle twenty feet above me. I can see the sky—a bird flashes across the circle. I suck in a shaky breath. Maybe I could stay here, in the dark, and it would be comfortable and safe, but I can see the sky.

I grip the ladder again. My foot takes a step.

"That's it, Keira, you've got it. One . . . two . . . three, up."

He keeps counting. My body keeps working, finding its determination. I'm still shaking and shivering and my mind is a tunnel even narrower than the one we're in, but I'm moving steadily upward now. The bright circle grows and grows.

"We've got this," Gable soothes as we move. "Don't you worry, we've got this."

And we have. Soon we're both climbing back out into the grungy courtyard. It could be a palace courtyard, for how happy I am to see it. My strength abandons me and I sprawl on the pavement. I breathe the air—real, fresh, whipped by wind, not held captive and stale underground—as Gable drags the manhole lid shut. He sits beside me, strokes my hair.

"You did it," he says. "I knew you could."

I just nod and close my eyes. Recover.

Breathe.

After that adventure, we can't stop. We take the metro to Montmartre and fulfill one of my life's ambitions: eat lunch at the café where *Amélie* was filmed. Gable buys me a painting from one of the artists hawking their wares. It's Notre Dame, painted in a Monet-like style, with big brush strokes and light, soft colors. Then, inspired, we go to Notre Dame. We climb the bell towers to the top. The wind tosses our hair and Gable kisses me in full view of the Parisian skyline.

As evening starts to fall, we grab some crêpes, and as I'm biting into my signature Nutella, I remember.

Levi.

"Shit, oh my God, Gable," I gasp, almost dropping my crêpe. "I told Levi I would be back at two. It's almost seven! *Shit*." I stand and whip out my phone for what must be the first time all day: seventeen missed calls from Levi. "I have to go back right fucking now."

"Could I . . . I mean, do you want me to come?" Gable asks. "I'll totally understand if you don't want me there, but . . ."

"No, come with me," I say. I'm terrified of what Levi will say—*have the hormones interfered with all your cognitive functions, you idiot?* Maybe he won't freak out in front of Gable.

We take the metro back to the Place d'Italie and walk up the street to Hoteltastique. All along the journey, I call Levi's phone, but it rings and rings and goes to voice mail every time, even though he was calling obsessively before. *God, Levi.*

When Gable and I are in the elevator, I realize that Levi might be wearing underwear or—gulp—even less. He might have vending machine snack wrappers all over the place, dirty socks tossed all over the floor, any manner of disgusting stuff.

"Um, I'd better go in first," I say when we get to our door.

When it's open, you can see down the center of the room, which includes the ends of the beds. The blankets are mussed up and thrown about, as usual, but Levi's feet aren't hanging off the end. A French cop show is on TV, the volume so loud it hurts. I step further into the room and turn off the TV.

Levi isn't in his bed. He isn't on the tiny balcony. I knock on the bathroom door and push it open, but he isn't there, either. His phone sits on the TV stand, screen lit up with all the missed calls from me.

"Levi?"

No answer.

My heartbeat batters at every pulse point like it could break my skin. I brace myself in the bathroom doorway as the fear builds.

Where the hell is he?

"Keira?" Gable calls. "Can I come in?"

"Um, yeah, yeah."

His shoes shuffle on the carpet. The front door bangs shut.

"Is something the matter?"

I nod. I can't stop sweeping my eyes over the bathroom. The sink. The bathtub. The bathmat.

"Levi's gone," I whisper. It echoes and I can't stand it. I back up, smack into Gable, but I'm too freaked to be dazed by more physical contact. "He's gone, he's not here. Where the fuck is he?"

"Did he go out for food?"

"He doesn't like going out alone, he would have waited for me, even if he was starving!"

"Okay, take deep breaths," Gable says, setting my painting carefully on the desk chair. "Deep breaths, yeah?"

I nod.

"Those are the shallowest breaths I've ever heard."

In, out. In, out.

In . . . out.

He squeezes my arm. "Okay?"

I nod.

"Now, if we're sure he's not here, we need to go downstairs and ask the front desk if they've seen him," he says in a calm, stable voice I couldn't hope to replicate.

I follow him back down the hall and to the elevator and almost jump when I see my reflection in the mirror. My skin is ghostly gray.

We approach the front desk, where the guy I think is the manager shuffles papers around and whistles. Gable looks at me, but when I don't make a move to speak, he asks the man, "*Excusez-moi, monsieur. Anglais?*"

He nods with a smile that feels so wrong.

"Have you seen my brother?" I ask. "H-he isn't in our room, and he's very unlikely to go anywhere on his own."

The man narrows his eyes, searching his memory.

"Tall?" he asks. He mimes muscular gorilla arms. "Big boy? Glasses?"

"Yes! Yes, that's him."

"He did leave," he says. "Perhaps two hours ago."

Gable grabs me by the arm before I even realize I'm falling backward. The manager's forehead is creased with a million lines.

"Is there something wrong?" he asks, eyes flicking between Gable and me.

"Yes," Gable says. "Her brother is . . . well, he has some mental issues, I think, and he doesn't know Paris very well—or at all."

The manager gives a curt nod and turns to address me. "*Mademoiselle*, do as much as you can to look for your brother," he says. "Check your room, check local shops. If the immediate area turns up nothing, we will contact the police directly."

I nod even though I want to shout *we need to call the police right now, right now, right now!* Levi doesn't just go places on his own, but I know you can't just jump to the conclusion of "missing" right away.

We return to the room with the manager, whose name is Yves, only because he insists we find any possible clue or lead. He opens the closet, as if Levi would just sit in there.

"Perhaps he went to the store?"

"No, he hasn't left our room in . . . like, a whole day. He was probably hungry. I was late coming back." I shake my head, but it doesn't clear the tears that block my throat.

"It's not your fault," Gable says.

The hell it's not.

I keep coming back to the bathroom. I don't know if I think he's just going to appear somehow—maybe I'm insane now. His toothbrush is here, his kiddie toothpaste is here, his colorful pills in their little dish are here. How could he not be here?

"Is this his?"

I whip around. Yves is holding up Levi's battered Star Wars wallet.

"Yes," I whisper.

He hands it to me and I wrench open the Velcro. Everything's still here. His debit card. The emergency credit card Mom insisted he carry. A single American dollar.

But no metro card.

"He took his metro pass," I murmur. If it's missing from his grubby wallet, he could be anywhere in Paris.

The next step: Gable and I run across the street to Margot and Nico's bakery.

The second I walk into the bakery, the bell above the door tinkles, and Margot emerges from the kitchen, drying her hands on a towel. Her pleasant smile folds into a look of alarm. "Keira, *mon Dieu*, what is wrong?"

I open my mouth but no words come out, until one does. "Levi."

"What?" She looks at Gable, and I can tell she immediately accepts him as part of the team.

"Levi is missing," Gable says.

Margot drops her dishtowel to the mosaic floor.

"*Non*," she says softly. "When last did you see him?"

"This morning, when I left to go meet Gable," I say on an inhale. "I was late getting home and I think he went out to look for food." Exhale. "H-he has his metro pass, he could be anywhere."

She covers her mouth with her hand. After a moment she says, "I haven't seen him. I'm so sorry."

I close my eyes. Her hand finds mine.

"Do not worry. We will do everything we can to help you."

# CHAPTER EIGHTEEN

We scour the immediate neighborhood, and when that turns up nothing, we go back to the bakery. Margot fires up the espresso machine. I sit with my phone in hand.

The equivalent of 911 in France is 112, but I can't seem to make my fingers dial. Is it the right time? Don't you have to wait twenty-four hours or something before you report someone missing? I'm sure there are exceptions to be made. I picture Levi's pills up in our room, doubting very much that he took ones he needs with him. He's out there, without medication, and I don't know what that means, but my throat closes up just thinking about it.

"Keira, you must call," Margot says softly, placing the steaming mocha in front of me. "The sooner, the better."

I nod. My eyes sting, blur, and a single tear drops onto the screen of my phone. I wipe it away.

"Should I call my mom first?"

"Police first," Nico says. He's been wringing his hands since he joined us.

"Your mom would probably want to know you're seeking help right away," Gable agrees. "You don't want her to panic."

"Yeah, you're right," I murmur.

My fingers finally pick out the three digits they need to dial.

They connect me to an English-speaking operator when my French fails. I tell the woman on the line everything. Brother, gone. Autism, mental illness, no meds. No knowledge of French or the area. The operator is very matter-of-fact. I tell her our names, the hotel we're staying at, where we are right now. She tells me she's dispatching police and the media will be alerted. She tells me to contact the American embassy.

When I hang up, my stomach unknots itself. Just a little.

"There you go," Margot says when I finally sip my drink. "Feel better?"

I nod, even though I don't. Not possible. Not when this is my fault.

Gable tries to rub my shoulder and calm me down, but I find myself edging away from him. I let him draw me away from Levi. How could I make this mistake again?

"Now call your *maman*," Margot reminds me gently.

All my breath comes shuddering out as I laugh weakly. "Do I have to?"

"If you don't, we will," Nico says with a grim smile.

I go to my contacts in TextAnywhere and hit CALL when I find her name. It rings twice before she answers.

"Hi, Keira!" Her voice is full of life for once. Even though it's, like, 5 a.m. in Shoreline.

I can't believe I have to ruin her this way.

"Mom," I say, and I hate how weak I sound. "I have something bad to tell you. Maybe you should sit down."

"What's going on, Keira? Is it—"

"Don't even guess," I tell her. "I'll just—I'll just say it. Levi is gone."

"Gone. Levi is . . . gone?"

"Yeah."

"What do you mean, *gone*?"

"I went up to our room and he isn't there. I was late coming home, and it's just not like him at all to go anywhere on his own. The manager of the hotel saw him leave a few hours ago but no one has seen him since. He doesn't have his phone."

"What?" she screams. "Why would he go? Have you called the police?"

"Yes, they're going to alert the media and do everything they can. We're going to form some kind of search party, too, and go all over the whole city if we have to."

Margot and Nico nod as I say these words. My heart melts at the determination in their eyes. Gable stares down at the tabletop, lips set into a firm line. I don't know what that means.

"Keira . . . this is . . . this is beyond words."

"I know. I'm so, so sorry, Mom. I've been doing really well looking after him, I swear, and I guess I just—"

She interrupts. "The only thing that matters right now is that we find Levi. Okay?"

"I don't know how much you can do from home, but if I think of anything, I'll let you know."

"Keira . . . I guess I have something to confess."

The worst words in existence.

"Josh and I . . . we aren't at home. We're in Paris. We're staying in the eleventh district."

I sit in silence. I can't decide if I'm too angry or too happy to speak.

"Keira? Keira, are you still there?"

"Yeah," I choke out. "How . . . why . . ."

"We left just after you did," she says, sounding rightly miserable. "It was my idea, I'm sorry. I was just . . . so, so scared."

"You assumed I was going to fuck up?"

"No! Josh and I thought it would be a good idea—"

"Don't blame Josh."

"—to have a base in Paris just in case," she says, ignoring me. "If anything happened, we would be a lot closer and able to help."

I swallow everything I want to scream at her. *You liar. You horrible, rotten liar. Why not just tell me?*

Instead, I focus on the tiny part of me that feels relief. "Just come meet me. I'm at Belliveau Pâtisserie in the 13th *arrondissement*."

Mom says she'll see me soon. I both hate and adore those words.

When I look up from my phone, everyone is staring at me.

"Turns out my mom and stepdad have been in Paris this whole time," I announce, slapping a fake smile on my face and shrugging. "Isn't that fabulous? Isn't that just great, that they didn't trust me to take care of my own brother?"

Except . . . they were right. They were right not to trust me, because it turns out I can't be trusted with Levi. My pretense erodes and I burst into tears. Margot stands and wraps me in her soft arms. She smells like mint and bread.

"*Tout sera d'accord*," she coos, stroking my hair. "It will all be okay. As soon as *maman et papa* arrive, we will start the search for Levi. Okay?"

I nod into her shoulder. It's all I want. To be out there, searching.

⤠⚮⤟

Two detectives arrive soon after. They introduce themselves as Inspector Bredoteau and Detective Giroux. They wear suits and frowns and their English is impeccable.

They stick to routine questions, where Levi might go (I don't know), what medications he takes (I go up and grab the bottles and recite the exact dosages for each pill), and what could happen if he goes without them for too long (I'm too scared to wonder). They ask if I have a photograph (I give them the one of him coughing next to a mime) and if I've phoned my parents yet.

"They're in Paris, it turns out," I say, sniffing away the last of my tears. "My mom and stepdad followed us here. They're on their way."

Mom and Josh arrive soon after. Seeing them walk into Margot and Nico's bakery, Shoreline meets Paris, feels like I've fallen into some kind of alternate reality.

Mom bursts into ugly tears when she sees me. She holds me too tight, crushing me against her frizzy hair, which is out of its perpetual ponytail. Her eyes are bloodshot and her nose is Rudolph red. Josh looks deadly grim, lips a thin, thin line. The wrinkle between his eyebrows, one of the only signs of age to touch him so far, has deepened tenfold since I last saw him. He squeezes my shoulder when we sit down at our table.

"Madame Braidwood, I'm Inspector Bredoteau and this is Detective Giroux," Bredoteau says. "We're glad you could get here so soon. We are going to do everything we can to locate your son, and being able to start early is a blessing."

Mom nods at them, and then her eyes travel to the others sitting at the table.

"Oh, Mom, this is Margot and Nico," I gesture. "They own this bakery. Levi and I have been coming here every day the whole trip so far."

Mom smiles at them, but sneaks a sideways glance at me. I can almost hear her thinking, *Bakery treats, every day? Hmmm.*

"It's great to meet you," she says, shaking Margot's hand and then Nico's.

"Anything you need of us, you have only to ask," Margot says with a shaky smile. "We will do anything we can."

Mom's lips tremble. "Thank you."

Then she looks at Gable.

"This is Gable McKendrick," I say. "He's a—a new friend."

I know right away that Mom knows what's up. My awkward introduction could only mean one thing.

My heartbeat races as the meeting goes on. We form a plan to make posters and start hanging them all over town. The police tell us alerts will go out to every department of law enforcement, to radio and TV stations, on the metro, social media, everything.

"Obviously, we cannot make guarantees," Bredoteau says, pained honesty in his eyes. "But I am confident that we can find Levi."

"There's no reason for him to run away," Mom says, mostly to herself. "He must have just decided to go for a walk and gotten lost. Right, Keira? Right?"

"I—I think so," I say.

What I don't say is "If there's a reason, it's me."

The detectives leave after promising to stay in constant contact. Nico sets up his computer and printer in the bakery seating area and gets to work on a poster of our own. He and Margot argue over the wording in French. Details like Levi's hair and eye colors, height, weight, and what he was last seen wearing are traded about the room. Finally, Nico prints it, and he and Josh rush out to find the nearest photocopier. The wheels have been set in motion.

I eat chocolate croissant after chocolate croissant during all this, and when the chocolate and pastry starts gluing my mouth closed, I move on to jam cookies and milk. Mom and Margot try to talk to each other while they wait for Josh and Nico, but Margot's English is too uncertain and Mom speaks not a word of French. She pronounces it "Bon-joo-er," for God's sake. I want to cover my eyes when I hear her try to repeat Margot's pronunciation of "mon fils," French for "my son."

"Moan feez," she keeps saying.

"Mon f-EESS," Margot repeats. "More, ah . . ."

"More emphasis on the S," I say to Mom. "And if you can't say the 'n' at the end of 'mon,' just skip it. 'Mo' sounds closer than 'moan.'"

Mom shoots subtle daggers at me. It looks like an even stare, just a cursory glance, but there's so much in that look. I just want to rest my head against the table and sleep, although I doubt I'd be able to with Gable drumming his fingers on the tabletop.

No. I just want to get out of here and search for Levi. Scour every metro station and tourist attraction, plaster the entire city in posters with his scowling face on them and repeat the words "*As-tu vu mon frère?*" a million times.

"Maybe there's a clue in the hotel room," Mom says.

"I've already searched the whole place. His wallet is there, minus his metro pass."

"He could be anywhere," she whispers.

"He wouldn't go just anywhere, Mom. He's not that adventurous. Believe me, I know."

She takes off her glasses and rubs her eyes. She murmurs, "Please stop, Keira."

"Please stop what?"

"Acting like you know everything," she says. "Being reductive, shutting down ideas like they're worthless. 'No, he wouldn't just go anywhere. No, there are only five specific places he could *possibly* go. You're *crazy* for thinking he could be *anywhere* else!'"

"Stop making that voice," I almost spit. "It's called using logic, Mom. Thinking logically about where he might go."

"And then, when he doesn't turn out to be in the places you so logically picked out for him, what then? We just give up, go home?" She scoffs. "I don't think so, Keira."

"When did I *ever* suggest giving up and going home? If we don't think logically and just shit our emotions out all over the place, how is that going to help us find him?"

"Sit, Keira," Margot says, hands on my shoulders. I didn't even realize I was on my feet. "You too, *Madame*."

"How could you lose him?" Mom says, turning away from me. Her shaking hand covers her eyes. "How could you, Keira?"

Petulant teenage words build up behind my teeth. I could say, "It wasn't my fault he ran away, how could I stop him?" I could scream and shout about how unfair this all is, about how they lied to me, and if they didn't trust me they shouldn't have let Levi come in the first place instead of lying to me. I could drudge up some crap about how if I was the one missing, no one would care. Past Me would have said all of this.

Present Me hates Mom all the more because everything she says is true. I wasn't trustworthy. I was stupid and air-headed and I neglected my brother because I wanted to have fun. And now look what happened, all because of me.

I'd rather die than tell her she's right for hating me.

"I want to go up to the hotel room," she says. "There must be some kind of clue up there."

"I'll come," I murmur. If she finds anything I've missed, she's just going to throw it in my face and use it as more evidence against me, but that's a fate I can't escape.

I almost forget Gable is still here. Mom and I head for the door and suddenly I see him, sitting there, half-drunk espresso in front of him.

"You don't have to stay for all this," I tell him. "You can go if you want to. I won't hate you for it."

If he goes, it's likely to be the end. I'll just be some girl he kissed in Paris whose brother went missing. Some crazy anecdote. It hurts, but I have to be okay with that.

He nods. Stays sitting.

"So . . ." I start, but he jumps in.

"I'm going to wait for your stepdad and Nico to bring the posters," he says. "I'll bring a stack with me. Help plaster the town."

It's my turn to wordlessly nod. I follow Mom outside and across the street to the hotel.

I introduce Mom to the hotel manager, Yves.

"How are things progressing?" he asks, worry lines all over his forehead.

"As well as can be hoped," I tell him. "I'll bring you some copies of the missing poster when it's done."

He nods repeatedly. "Please, please do."

We have a long wait while the elevator takes its sweet time getting down to the lobby. Mom runs her fingers through her hair and stares blankly ahead at the wall. I tap my shoe just for something to do. The elevator lights show that it's still three floors above us.

"What have you guys been doing in Paris so far?" I ask gently. I'm treading on very thin ice.

"Nothing," Mom says. "We don't have the money to enjoy the sort of vacation you're taking."

It stings like acid to the face. The sort of vacation *I'm* taking . . . I worked my ass off to save the money for this trip. I earned it. I deserve it. I want to tell her "You didn't have to come here," but, if I want to keep my head, I can't exactly say things like that to a mother with a missing child right now.

We step into the elevator and say no more until we get to the room.

"It stinks in here," Mom says, walking immediately toward the window. "Let's get some fresh air flowing."

She opens the curtains and the window and starts poking through Levi's things the same way I did, and she finds nothing I didn't find already. His wallet. *The Billionaire Rancher's Bride*. His cell phone, sitting on the TV stand. She sighs.

"Kind of a pipe dream that he would take it with him," she says, touching it.

I nod and step into the bathroom, closing the door. I've been vaguely aware of the fact that I've had to pee for a while, and now the urge is overwhelming. I lift the toilet lid and that's when I notice something.

A tiny pill, semi-dissolved, sticks to the side of the bowl.

I grab Levi's pill tray. All the ones leading up to today are gone, as usual.

But if that pill is down there . . . I'm willing to bet they all are.

Mom sighs in the next room. Bedsprings creak as she sits down.

I'm frozen.

She'll scream at me. She'll berate me for being a complete, utter moron. I could tell, when she saw Gable, that she was wondering how she could've ended up with such an airhead for a daughter. Who goes on a trip and acquires a boyfriend? The same daughter who accidentally leaves the milk on the counter after pouring it into her cereal. The same daughter who once walked into the sliding glass door and ended up on the floor with everyone laughing while she suppressed tears. The one who once forgot to lock the car for a five-minute grocery run, giving someone the perfect opportunity to steal Mom's iPod and Josh's expensive headphones. The one who was always conveniently unavailable when the family needed her, when her brother needed her, because who wanted to deal with difficult feelings when she could bask in the glory of Jacques St-Pierre and his smirk instead? That daughter was willfully blind, willfully ignorant. She skipped out on her family.

That idiot daughter couldn't keep on her brother to take his meds, didn't even think to watch him swallow them and check underneath his tongue. Big surprise. She can't do anything right.

I squeeze my eyes shut. If I don't tell her, it's bad for me, but it's even worse for Levi. She needs to know. The police need to know.

"M-mom?"

"Yes?"

"Come here."

She walks slowly to the bathroom. Her face looks puffy and bleary in the yellow vanity lights as her eyes follow my pointing finger.

"What is . . ." Sharp intake of breath. "Oh my God, Keira."

My grip tightens on the edge of the sink. Levi is out there with no medication in his body. God only knows when he last swallowed a pill.

Judging by Mom's soft sobs, that's something to be very, very afraid of.

# CHAPTER NINETEEN

Mom called Josh first, luckily getting him before they photo-copied the posters. Josh added "Off his medications, may be confused or hallucinating" to the bottom and Nico scrawled the French translation. When the sky is dark, we finally have posters to distribute. I'm starting to feel exhausted, but now is not the time for rest.

All through the night, we paint the town with posters: taping them up in the window of every shop, fixing them to every street light, descending into the metro stations and handing them out to people on the last legs of their commutes. We see teams in the metro stations, plastering official Interpol posters all over. When we finally turn in after midnight, Josh, Mom, and I congregate in my and Levi's hotel room and watch TV. The local French news stations broadcast the story of a lost American boy in Paris. Mom quietly sobs.

Gable had worked through the night with us, and my hotel offered him a free room just like they did for Mom and Josh, but he quietly refused.

"I need to go," he said. "I'll put up a poster in my hostel, okay?"

I nodded. He kissed my forehead and left.

I'm trying not to think about him.

Mom cries herself to sleep in Levi's bed. Josh sits up with me, watching the news anchor make his way through the night's stories, just waiting for Levi to be mentioned again.

"How has the trip been?" Josh asks, quiet so as not to wake Mom. She's a light sleeper.

"Fine," I mutter, turning my phone over and over in my hands. "I mean . . . not perfect."

"Everything you dreamed of?"

Tears sting my eyes. I reach for the box of tissues Mom had been clinging to.

"Everything's different," I whisper.

Josh doesn't say anything else. He just waits.

"Being with Levi is hard sometimes," I tell him. "It really, really sucks to be around someone who's actively *trying* to hurt you. He gets in these moods where he's determined to make me feel awful, to push every single one of my buttons. He'll insult things I like, or just straight-up call me stupid to my face—he has no problem doing that."

Josh nods. I keep going.

"Why does he have to do that? He threw a fit at Versailles because he didn't want to admire a place he said was built on the backs of 'the People,' with a capital P."

Josh's eyes crinkle in a smile. "That's Levi. Our red menace."

My laugh is lost in another tiny sob. "But then . . . even though he pisses me off, I sort of admire the way he thinks. Mom will tell you it's all because something's been off with his brain chemistry this whole time, but it can't just be that. You can't write off every aspect of someone's personality and explain it all away with an illness. Right?"

Josh sighs. "Your mom wants to find reasons. She doesn't want to believe Levi means the things he says and the things he does. Sometimes he scares her."

"He's just not like her. That's what she doesn't like. I'm not her, either."

"Hey," he says. "Don't think she doesn't love you, like, an insane amount. She does."

"A lot of the time it sure doesn't feel like it."

He squeezes my shoulder. "You're growing up. I think both Levi and Mom are having trouble with that."

I just nod, pretending I'm getting the message.

"We should both get some sleep," he says. "Can I leave her in here with you?"

"Yeah, of course."

"Goodnight, Keir. Everything will be better in the morning."

But how can it be?

I leave Mom sleeping on Levi's bed. I brush my teeth, change into my pajamas, turn off the TV, and slip under the covers, but sleep doesn't come. I stare into the darkness, thinking about Levi and where he might be. The night is brisk and his coat is still thrown over the chair in the corner. Is he shivering? Is he sleeping, or staying up all night? A tired, weak Levi might be easier to find. A tired, weak Levi might even come home.

I watch the glow-in-the-dark hands on Levi's alarm clock turn. He's been gone for ten, eleven, twelve, thirteen hours now. Fourteen. Fifteen . . . it's seven in the morning now and I haven't slept a wink. With a heavy sigh, I get up to use the bathroom. My foot hits the floor between the two beds but instead of the old carpet, my toes land on a piece of paper.

I turn on the bedside lamp. Mom's arm hangs over the side of the bed and this bit of paper looks like it fell from her hand. I pick it up, and as I'm unfolding it, I realize what it is.

Levi's suicide note. Mom carried it all the way here.

I almost drop it again. I almost push it under the bed, out of sight, out of mind. The old me would get up and act like she'd never even saw it. I don't, though. I dodged it before when I thought I was above this pain, but now I need it.

*Mom,* it says at the top, in Levi's shaky child's printing. The letter blurs in front of my eyes almost the second I start to read.

*Im sorry I was a bad son. I didnt try very hard. You were nice and did a good job and tried. Its ok that dad is gone because you are a good mom so dont worry about that.*

*Tell Keira that shes the best sister ever and I love her. Im sorry I bug her and I think she doesnt like me anymore. You should tell her to go to Paris even if she doesnt want to anymore once I am gone. I think maybe she belongs there and will be happy.*

*Bye,*

*Levi*

The childish writing, such horrible words. Such small, unhappy words, like a knife to the heart. This can't be real. These can't really be the words he chose to leave us with. So weak. So . . . honest. This isn't the Levi I know—the sullen, sarcastic Levi. This is a young kid, no calloused outer shell.

This is Levi, on the inside.

I force myself to read it again and again.

*I think she doesnt like me anymore.*

In my head, I compose a reply.

*It's not true, Levi. Maybe I didn't realize it sometimes, but you're the best thing in my life. You're my brother, the only one I have. The only other one who understands what it's like to be in this family. You're my partner in crime. You share all my history. Sure, sometimes you're a raincloud, but everybody is a raincloud sometimes, Lev. If you bugged me, it was only because you were trying to remind me what's important. I've forgotten what's important, Lev. Boys, foreign cities, adventure . . . none of them could ever come close to you. None of them is a replacement for you. None of them is even a cheap imitation of you. You needed me—but you still wanted the best for me, wanted me to be happy—and I wasn't there. Now I know I need you just as badly. Where are you?*

*Where are you, Levi?*

Light starts to push past the curtains and birds chirp outside. Not songbirds making pretty noise like in Shoreline. These are harsh crow's caws and the cooing of pigeons, but it's all the same. Morning is here and I can only think about Levi, sniffing in the cold, hands tucked into his hoodie pockets, wandering the streets. Maybe they'll find him soon. Who else will be out on the streets at that time? Maybe he'll be spotted on the metro. Maybe, right now, someone is sitting with him after phoning the police, reassuring him that help is on the way, to take him home. Maybe someone is dialing the missing person's line right now.

I start counting the seconds. Surely, if there's a report that he'd been seen, they'll phone us right away. Right? Josh will come and pound on the door, shouting for us to wake up.

But nothing happens as I count *un, deux, trois*. No relieved voices, no ringing phones. Only Mom's snores and the faint sound of a TV in another room.

I grab my purse and sneak out of the room after leaving a note for Mom. I'm restless, on high alert.

When I push open the bakery door and the little bell dings, I'm greeted by the only thing that could comfort me: the smell of baking bread. I breathe in deeply and I can feel my whole body shudder in relief. Margot sticks her head out of the kitchen and smiles sadly when she sees me.

"No Levi," she says. It's not a question; she knows.

I shake my head. "Nothing at all yet."

"The police will be here soon—they will be working from here." She disappears back into the kitchen and reemerges with a stack of baguettes. "Do you like our window?"

The front window is covered in posters, and in the very middle the words AS-TU VU CE GARÇON? are painted in bold lettering.

"Thank you so much," I tell her. "It's amazing."

She nods. "Nico is leading a neighborhood search party leaving from here at 9. The people, they are being so helpful. Now, you need a strong breakfast."

"A baguette would be good. I'll take that up to my mom. And um, *pain au chocolat pour moi, s'il vous plaît?*"

"Sit, sit. I will bring it to you."

I sit at our table, where just a couple days ago, we poured over brochures. My eyes were full of stars and my head was full of possibilities, and Levi only wanted to shoot me down. Why? Why couldn't he just calm down and shut his mouth for an afternoon? Why didn't he enjoy those places like I did? We went on a road trip with Mom and our grandparents when we were young, before Josh, and Levi loved The Alamo. He insisted Mom buy him every Alamo-related thing in the gift shop. We still have an Alamo pencil sharpener kicking around in the junk drawer, and Levi still has an Alamo poster on his bedroom wall and a scale model on his desk. Why couldn't he feel that same reverence for Versailles, Notre Dame, or the Louvre? Why couldn't he tolerate the things I loved?

I sit and think, think hard, about where he would go in this city, given the choice.

Somewhere he doesn't hate, presumably. Some place associated with Hitler? Somewhere associated with some communist movement in France or something? Was there ever even a communist movement here?

It's got to be somewhere he feels comfortable. Or somewhere that interests him but doesn't threaten him.

When Margot sets down two buttery, shining croissants in front of me, and lays a bagged, still-steaming baguette across the table, it hits me.

Levi felt threatened.

In all the places where he threw fits, he felt threatened. When Levi gets to choose his surroundings, he goes for quiet, solitary places, like his basement bedroom. And quiet, solitary places have been hard to come by on this trip. We've been in enormous cathedrals and squares and palaces, and they've all been full of soaring, open space. That sets my heart on fire, but it makes Levi cower.

And then there's Gable, and Gable basically took away something that always feels safe to him: me. When I was off with Gable, Levi felt that he had to go in search of safety.

I pull the brochures out of my bag and helplessly paw through them as I chew the flaky flesh of my croissant. He wouldn't go to any of the places on these glossy brochures. He would pick somewhere out of the way.

My metro map peeks out from under the brochures and I open it. The colored lines I've stared at for years, planning trips in my dreams, are as good a place to start as any.

There are all the places we've been already. The Palais Royale Musée du Louvre stop. Place Denfer-Rochereau. The one near us, the Place d'Italie.

And then I stumble upon one stop, in the upper left quadrant of the map, across the Seine from the Eiffel Tower. The stop called Franklin D. Roosevelt.

Levi pointed to it and asked what was there. I brushed it off.

I wonder . . .

I stuff the other, uneaten croissant into the same paper casing the baguette is in and dash out the door.

"See you later, Margot!" I call over my shoulder.

She shouts something to me but I don't hear. I don't have time.

I run up to the hotel room. Miraculously Mom is still asleep and isn't woken by my thundering around the room, getting dressed. I wrap the uneaten croissant in a napkin and shove it into my jacket pocket as I sneak out the door again, metro pass in hand. I might need it to lure Levi, like a stray, untrusting dog.

It's a long ride to Franklin D. Roosevelt. When I emerge from the underground onto the street, I realize I'm on the Champs

Élysées. There's a massive roundabout in the Place de Franklin D. Roosevelt, and then the wide thoroughfare of Champs Élysées continues toward the Arc de Triomphe in the distance.

If Levi came here, was he disappointed? He was probably looking for some relic of American history, some measure of familiarity in Paris. There's nothing here but an average block of the Champs Élysées. I imagine him looking up the street at the distant Arc de Triomphe and feeling the same pull toward it that I feel.

Of course he would have. It's like gravity.

The street is empty and the Arc is far, far away. I walk for blocks and it remains a phantom structure, stark against the sky, dove gray in the morning. Finally, the sun emerges and bathes it in glorious light.

Paris comes to life around me. Shoppers emerge from metro stations like gophers popping out of the ground. Cars swoop up and down the street and fling themselves into roundabouts. A busker plays "Can You Feel the Love Tonight?" on an accordion and I toss a Euro into his hat.

I'm sweating by the time the Arc looms above me, actual and attainable. Tour buses are already parked nearby, visitors crossing the busy roundabout into the Arc's shelter. People pose for pictures, making peace signs and scrunching their faces up in awkward smiles.

The Arc de Triomphe is blindingly bright. The sun hits the white stone and reflects off the carved images of Victory. Walking under the arch, into the deep shade the sun hasn't touched yet, I wonder if my stupid hunch is really any use at all or if I'm deluding myself.

I miss Levi. Even if he was grumbling and complaining most of the time. And hey, what would the world be if no one looked at it critically? If no one ever pointed out the shitty things in life, we would all just stumble around in a constant state of idiotic admiration. Nothing would ever get done.

You need a healthy dose of cynicism. And the cynics need a healthy dose of wide-eyed wonderment every once in a while. Levi and I, we work off each other. Balance each other out. We need each other.

Then I see him.

Levi sits on a park bench across the roundabout, squinting in the sunshine, hands in his pockets. He hasn't seen me.

My mind shuts down. My body takes over.

I find the nearest crosswalk and wait for the cars to stop. They don't.

I can't lose him. I can't let this slip away.

I run. Gallop in front of cars when they slam on their brakes. Double back and go around when a car gets in my way. It's a high-speed, high-stakes game of Frogger. Or chess, deciphering the way the cars move and trying to beat them. Checkers, when I almost have to vault over the hood of a car that stops directly in front of me. Musical chairs, with all the honking that follows me.

I lose sight of Levi for a fraction of a second. He's gotten up from the bench and wandered further into the park, hunched forward and shuffling. My heart lurches—he *cannot* get away from me.

A Smart Car barrels toward me, honking, and I jump to the safety of the sidewalk just in time—but my toe hooks on the edge of the curb. I fall.

I land on my right hand, and I feel something crunch in there. My arms skid along the cement. They tear and bleed and sting, little bits of gravel stuck in the wounds. My knees ache sharply under freshly torn jeans. It takes a minute before my breath returns and I can get up.

"*Ça va?*" a voice asks. "Oh, you are bleeding!"

"*Ça va,*" I repeat. "I'm fine, I'm fine . . ."

I look around for Levi. Fuck, I can't have lost him again. There's his bench, that's the direction he was walking in . . .

Oh.

He's stopped. He's staring at me, a squinting, still figure about a hundred feet away, in his T-shirt, sweatpants, and boots. Don't look away, Levi. Don't run. Don't, don't . . .

He doesn't.

I get to my feet, brush the gravel off my hands—*big mistake,* my wrist explodes in pain—and go to him. I'm almost terrified to reach him, but my legs keep moving and now I'm jogging. He doesn't move a muscle. If this were a movie, the soundtrack would soar to a crescendo. I would run in slow-motion, my face stretched in agony. My momentum would carry me straight into him, and he would wrap me up in a big, brotherly bear hug and say something silly like "Hiya, sis!" The sight of us would warm the hearts of many a passerby.

In real life, I stop in front of Levi, panting and bleeding. My knees flare with pain.

He blinks.

"Did you see me almost get hit by a SmartCar?"

He doesn't say anything.

"I'd give it an eight out of ten, myself," I say, still panting.

His face remains blank.

"I'm glad to see you," I tell him. "I've been so worried, Levi."

Nothing.

I turn and look at the Arc de Triomphe, somehow even grander at a distance than when you're beneath it.

"It's pretty cool, huh?"

Nothing.

"We should've come to see it earlier."

More silence. So many questions sit in the space between us and set up camp there. His eyes are hazy and I remember: no drugs. I feel like I'm walking on eggshells.

My wrist burns on the inside. A droplet of blood drips from my arm. It stains the pavement beside my foot. "Um, I think I need some medical attention," I say to the droplet.

He still doesn't say anything.

"But first I should call Mom." I bite my lip. "She and Josh are here, in Paris."

Levi blinks. I'm not sure if he heard me. He sits down on the bench behind us and continues to stare at the Arc innocently, mildly, like he hasn't a care in the world. I sit next to him and hold my hands out in front of me like a zombie to keep from bleeding on my clothes.

I can't get out my phone, the way my wrist aches, and I don't want to break the silence. So I just keep sitting here. Passersby look at us a bit funny. I want to ask for help. I want someone to ask if I'm okay, and I'll tell them no and ask them to get out my phone and call Mom. Maybe someone will recognize Levi from the posters (please, please, please). I can see his surly face staring at us from a lamp post a few meters away. A dog pauses to pee on the pole and his owner stands there, looking around. I will him to look at the poster and then at us. Poster, then us, please, sir.

The man's eyes land on me as I'm staring. The dog finishes peeing and kicks at the ground, ready to move on, but I mouth "Help!" The man furrows his brow and tilts his head. I point, with my bleeding hand, at the poster next to him. His face goes white at the blood, and I keep pointing until he finally looks.

He puts it together and gets out his cell phone. He calls the number on the poster and has a brief conversation, in French, where I can pick out my brother's name and the words *"Arc de Triomphe avec une fille . . . sa soeur? Oui, peut-être . . ."*

He flips his phone shut after giving more directions. I smile my gratitude and he nods. His dog becomes really interested in the grass across the way, and the man throws a ball for the little terrier and keeps an eye on us until the police come.

When they arrive, talking loudly and ushering Levi and me into a police car, it feels like I've finally stepped back from a ledge I'd been standing on for hours, days.

Levi is safely in our hands.

That's all I wanted, this whole time, but when the police come, my new fear is that Levi will freak out. Get angry, frustrated with all the noise, turn on me for turning him in. He won't understand that I had to do it. He won't understand any of this. That's my fear.

What really happens? Levi cooperates. No fight. No curiosity as to what's going on. He just clutches my sleeve and follows me. He's a zombie.

He rests his head against the window of the police car as we speed off and I notice something clutched in his hand. I carefully ease it out.

A piece of our hotel's stationery, with my scrawled words across it: *Went out for a bit, back around 2—Keira*

# Chapter Twenty

At the hospital, they whisked Levi off and left me in the emergency room where a doctor took one look at my wrist and pronounced it sprained. As a nurse was binding it, my knee started to twinge and throb. The nurse rolled up my pant leg and immediately yelled for the doctor. Apparently my kneecap had taken up residence toward the outside of my leg. The doctor merrily pushed it back into place. I puked into a wastebasket.

And then they left me while they waited for Mom and Josh. Now, I'm alone with the words:

*Tell Keira that shes the best sister ever and I love her.*

*I think she doesnt like me anymore.*

*Went out for a bit, back around 2.*

The best sister ever. Levi really must be deluded.

When they arrive at the hospital, Mom goes to Levi and Josh comes to me in the E.R.

"Hey, King Tut," he says, nodding at all my bandages.

I give him a look and he chuckles his signature Josh chuckle.

"Just messing with you, kid," he says. He sits down in the chair next to my bed and exhales probably the longest breath I've ever heard. "God, it's sure a relief to be able to make jokes again."

"How is he?" I ask, afraid to hear his answer.

"Asleep right now, and probably will be for quite a while. He's pretty cold, couldn't stop shivering. And he's getting his meds back into his system. But, eventually, he's going to be fine."

It's my turn to sigh the biggest sigh known to man.

"I was so stupid, Josh," I whisper. "This was—"

"Don't let me hear you say 'this was all my fault.' It wasn't."

"But—"

"And I won't let you say otherwise, Keira. Levi chose not to take his meds. You couldn't have controlled that, even if you tried."

"But I could have been there," I murmur to my hands in my lap. "I *should* have been there. Instead I wanted to spend time with a stupid boy. He—he had this in his hand when I found him." I shove my stupid, lying note into Josh's hand. "I was late. He must have gone out looking for me."

Josh reads the note over and over, his eyebrows knitting together. He's going to freak out, I can tell. Yell at me. "Hey," he says, his voice all sad and soft. I realize there are tears running down my face. "Don't cry, Keir. No one could blame you for wanting to spend time with a boy. Sure, maybe you could've done things differently, but none of us has a time machine."

I sniff back tears. "He was so . . . so distant when I found him. Like a ghost."

"You didn't do that to him, Keira. His own brain does that to him. Don't beat yourself up over this."

"Don't let Mom hear you say that," I warn him, wiping my tears with my bandages. "She wants to kill me, I know she does."

"Hey, look." He pauses. "No, really, look at me."

I do. His eyes are wide and honest. For the billionth time, I say a silent prayer of thanks that Mom met him.

"She isn't angry with you," he says.

"How do you know?"

"Because what have you done since this mess started? *You looked for him.* You didn't give up hope."

"But that's the most basic thing," I say. "Who would give up? 'Oh, looks like my brother's missing, I'll just lie down and die now.'"

"Keira, be serious."

Anyone would be a complete and utter lame-ass for not doing the bare minimum I did. Really, I could've done so much more. Not gotten frustrated with Levi for his brain chemistry. Had a little more sensitivity. Realized he's been ill all along. Zombie Levi, who I saw today? That's who he was for years. If I'd sensed the wrongness earlier, spent some time with him like he so desperately wanted, maybe he wouldn't have tried to kill himself. He'd be a whole lot better off.

"All I'm saying is to stop beating yourself up for not being more than human," Josh says. "We couldn't have asked any more of you."

I politely disagree, silently.

Josh gently pats my leg, careful to steer clear of my knee. "If anything is anyone's fault, it's mine."

"Hey, if I'm not allowed to take blame, you *definitely* aren't."

"No, really," he says. "I know Levi's always resented me. He barely *acknowledges* me, and it's been how many years now? I should've tried harder to win him over. Tried to change his mind about me."

I've never heard heartbreak in Josh's voice before. Right now, as his downcast eyes search my bedspread like it has the answers, it's the first time I've ever seen him be anything other than calm, laid-back. That uncertainty doesn't belong in his eyes. I shake my head so hard it almost hurts.

"Never mind what Levi thinks," I say. "You're the best thing that's ever happened to any of us. I've been trying to convince him for years."

Josh shakes his head. He smiles faintly. "Keep trying for me. God knows you're the only one he'll listen to."

I reach over and hug him.

"I'll wear him down eventually," I tell him. "I promise."

⚜

I'm not sure if I'm stuck in the hospital for my own sake, or because they're still working on Levi. Josh stays with me, trying to keep me entertained, but I don't see Mom for a few hours. When she comes into my little curtained-off area, her eyes are sunken pits, red from tears, and her ponytail is even frizzier than usual. Josh stands and takes her hand.

"What's the news?" he asks.

"Bloodwork came back," Mom says, her voice unsteady. "He—he hasn't been taking his medication, probably not since leaving treatment. That's *weeks* of flushing pills."

I have to stop her from saying any more. "I don't need you to tell me it's all my fault."

She looks up at me. Deadly silence fills the space between the hospital curtains.

I continue. "Believe me, I fucking know. How do you think I feel, knowing you were right? I can't be trusted with Levi—I can't be trusted with *myself*. I've been, like, two seconds away from a mental breakdown this whole trip. How the *hell* could I ever take care of Levi?"

I only realize I had this fear when it comes spilling out of my mouth in a shrill, unhinged screech. Tears fill my eyes. Mom is silent. I can't see her anymore through the blur.

"I've told her, Amanda," Josh whispers. "I've told her it's not her fault, that we don't blame her, but—"

Mom turns and walks away, shoes squeaking on the hospital linoleum. I grab the cheap, flat pillow off my hospital bed, bury my face in it, and scream. It doesn't do shit to absorb the sound.

"Keira, it's okay." Josh sits beside me and wraps an arm around my shoulders. "She's under a lot of stress right now. She needs some time to process everything."

My tears and snot soak the pillow. Some time? I don't think a thousand years could change the fucked-up way we are.

"You're too hard on yourself," Josh says. "Give yourself some credit, okay, kid? It's so hard to hear you beat yourself up."

I nod numbly. Josh squeezes my shoulder one last time.

"Want some baguette?" he asks, producing half a baguette wrapped in paper out of nowhere. "I was skeptical at first, but man, I've been living off plain bread since we got here. This stuff is the *shit*."

My lip twitches with the ghost of a smile. I rip off a chunk of slightly stale bread. It tastes like nothing, but I chew and swallow anyway. I will do anything for the parent who will sit with me while I cry instead of running out of the room.

❦ ❦

I manage to take a fractured nap, full of hospital noises and far from satisfying. When I'm in a drowsy half-sleep, a heavy weight lands on the edge of my bed. A hand squeezes my shoulder and I glance up.

It's Mom.

"Are you okay, baby?" she asks. She tucks a lock of hair behind my ear, and my skin almost stings where her fingers brush.

I sit up. She looks haggard, like a million worries have landed on her shoulders and her body is digesting them all. Her hair is greasy in its perpetual ponytail, her skin is breaking out, her eyes are red and puffy. She looks the way she used to when she was dragging Levi and me around town on errands and listening to us scream and make demands in the supermarket and then cry when we weren't appeased. My brain says *proceed with caution, screaming imminent*, but Mom smiles hesitantly. At me.

Something inside me breaks like a dam. I bite down on my wobbling lip when Mom holds out her arms. I sink into them. She rocks me back and forth and I just want to tell her everything. Every little worry I've had on this trip, every insecurity that has ever dwelled in my brain, I want to offer them all up to her and have her crush them to dust in the soft hands she runs over my hair.

"I'm sorry I walked away," she whispers.

"It's okay," I say, because it's what I'm supposed to say, even if it's not okay.

"No, it's not. I was so angry at the situation with Levi, and when you accused me of blaming you, I was just so angry I couldn't speak. Not angry at you," she says hastily. "Angry with myself."

"With yourself?"

I feel her nod against me. "Because I have blamed you in the past. I've turned a blind eye when it comes to you, in general, especially the past few months. I convinced myself that helping Levi was more important. I . . . I saw some signs of trouble with you, but I . . . well, I pretended I didn't. Part of me thought your problems were your own to deal with, and now I realize how stupid it was for me to think that."

I want to tell her it's okay, don't worry about it, but I can only sit here, dumbfounded.

"You remind me of myself, Keira," Mom admits. "In more ways than I can count. You fight so hard you exhaust yourself, and you only cry for help when it's almost too late. You blame yourself for everything, you throw yourself on the fire. That frustrates me because it's what I do, too. My instinct was always to get angry, instead of teaching you to stop taking on all this guilt."

She sounds like she's reading from a self-help book, but the truth of her words settles into me like a nourishing meal. Her honesty feels like a kick in the gut—in a good way, if that's possible. I have no idea what to say, so I just say, "It's okay, Mom."

"It's not okay. You think you're the problem here, and I should never, ever have let you think that. I'm sorry, Keira. I was scared. Finding out that Levi's been tricking me and lying to me about taking his pills is even scarier."

I just nod.

"So I'm sorry," she says. She finally releases me from her embrace. "You aren't to blame. Levi is his own worst enemy."

"But he's my responsibility."

"He's all of our responsibility," she says, "but you are not his parent. You're his sister. That's important—crucial, even—but you are *not* to blame. Okay?"

I nod, maybe not believing her, but willing to try.

She takes my hand and squeezes it. Hers is cold and dry, probably from loading up on hospital hand sanitizer. "How have you been feeling?"

I held up my bandaged wrist. "Sore. My knee, too. Plus I have all these scrapes and—" I think of everything that's happened to me on this trip: the museum episode, my panic in the dark catacombs. The tightness in my chest, the fear and anxiety over how close Levi came to being gone . . . "—and I was under a lot of stress, the past few days. I'm okay, though. Or I will be soon."

Mom smiles and reaches into her purse for a tissue. She hands me one, too, and we mop up the remnants of our tears while laughing. I can't take my eyes off her. I've suddenly realized what a miracle it is that she's here, in Paris.

"What do you think of Paris, Mom?" I ask her. "Or what you've seen, anyway."

She doesn't answer for a moment as she folds her tissue into a tiny square. When she speaks, it's a whisper: "It's incredible, Keira. Can you make me a promise?"

"Um, sure."

"Promise we'll come back, all four of us, and see it all together?"

I grin. "Easiest promise I've ever made."

⚬✦⚬ ⚬✦⚬

I go back to the hotel on crutches, once the doctor has put a brace on my knee and given me a strict warning to be careful or else he'll come find me in America and force me to rest it. I think he was trying to be funny, but it came off as vaguely threatening. Josh and I laugh about it for something to do, but there's no disguising the fact that we're missing Mom and Levi, who are still at the hospital.

"Get some rest, Keira," Josh says as I hobble to my room. He opens the door for me. "This will all look better in the morning."

The morning. We have a flight booked. We're going home.

I don't know how I feel about that. I do understand that, yeah, Levi needs to go home. He needs to see his doctors. He needs a full-arsenal effort to try to figure out how to help him. I feel like the biggest idiot for ever denying that now. My brain tries to tell me I couldn't have known how serious his problems were until I saw them with my own eyes, that I never got the full blast of his condition. I was sheltered.

My heart tells me I'm the shittiest person alive for never trying to become *un*sheltered. It was easy to deny, and I'm lazy. I will always pick the easy route even when it comes to my brother. Who I love more than anything.

But then I think of Marie Antoinette. You can't always blame people for their ignorance, for the circumstances of their lives. It's not always something they can control, and the full truth of the world's awfulness isn't always something they can handle.

I'm wiping up tears yet again when my phone rings. It's Gable.

"Hey," he says when I answer. "I heard you found Levi."

"Yeah, at the Arc de Triomphe. He stayed the night in a park."

"Is he okay?"

I swallow. "He will be."

"Good." He pauses. "Are *you* okay?"

"Just a sprained wrist and dislocated kneecap, but nothing rest won't fix. I would never let a SmartCar take me out."

"*What?* I meant emotionally—what the bloody hell are you talking about?"

"Oh! I almost got hit by a SmartCar. I jumped out of the way in time, though. It's all good."

"That sounds intense."

"It was. Sort of badass, though."

"I can imagine."

Awkward silence. I fiddle with my knee brace while I wait for him to say something, anything. I don't want to talk.

"So, shot in the dark," Gable continues, "but I'm going home to Edinburgh tomorrow, and I was sort of wondering if you'd maybe like to come along? It could just be for a few days, even, while your family works out what you guys are doing. I don't know. I realize now that it's a stupid idea, and you're one-hundred-percent free to shoot me down, but . . ."

A few days ago, this invitation would have been the best, most fairy-tale thing to ever happen to me. I would've been shaking, just imagining the wind-swept highlands and the craggy mountains and myself conquering that rugged land.

But, right now, in Scotland with a cute boy is not where I need to be.

"We actually have a flight home booked for tomorrow," I murmur.

"Oh," he says. "Right. Of course."

More silence. What is there to say?

"If I'm ever in Scotland, I'll give you a shout?"

"Yeah, yeah, totally," he says. "I'd like to see you again, Keira. We had a good time."

"Yeah, we did."

"Well . . . add me on Facebook?"

I grin. "Of course."

So we say "so long, see you someday," and then hang up. I log into Facebook and find Gable McKendrick. His profile picture has him on a mountainside, posing with a bunch of other kids who must be his siblings and a lady in the middle who must be his mother. They're all wearing kilts. The lump in my throat swells.

I like Gable. He's sweet and funny and genuinely seems to care about me. But the time and place are so, so wrong.

But hey, if I ever go to Scotland, I have a couch to sleep on. I've always read that, in the world of travel, that one thing can be worth its weight in gold.

And anyway, there's always "someday."

◦✑◦ ◦✑◦

The next morning, I peek out the curtains at the rooftops across the way. Neighborhood cats hold a cranky congregation, the birds chirping teasingly above them. A girl speeds by on a Vespa. An old man at the local newsstand smokes a cigar and frowns at the front pages of the papers.

I'm going to miss this place. No hostel by the Seine could have done any better.

Even though I'm on my stupid crutches, I can't let my morning tradition slip by, not on the last chance I'll get.

I hobble down to the bakery. It takes twice as long as usual, but I'd go three times as far for Margot and Nico's croissants.

This time, there's a woman ahead of me in line, ordering a baguette and two *pains aux chocolat*. She smiles at me and tells me she's glad I found my brother. A very serious-looking old man in a bowler hat sits at Levi's and my table with a jam cookie and espresso. And Margot beams as she comes around the counter to hug me.

"You look so happy," I say into her ear as she squeezes me gently.

"You have helped make it so," she whispers. "*Merci, merci, merci.*"

"Thank *you*," I tell her, "for filling our time here with sweetness."

I can't believe such greeting-card cheesy words just came out of my mouth, but Margot seems to like it. She finally lets me go with one last squeeze. She wipes a tear from her cheek when we finally pull apart.

"Thanks to you," she says, "I have met someone very special. Come!"

She leads me toward the older gentlemen in the bowler hat. He stands up. His eyes twinkle under bushy, wild eyebrows.

"*Voici* Monsieur Goldberg," she says. "He is the nephew of the neighbor my *grandpère* gave refuge to in this very *pâtisserie*."

I shake Monsieur Goldberg's hand. It's papery and dry, but his smile is bright and warm.

"*Merveilleux de vous recontrez*," I stutter.

"*Toi aussi*," he says. "Thanks to the news story of your brother being found, I was finally able to locate the bakery that was next to my uncle's apartment. I saw this street on the news and recognized it from the old photos."

"That's amazing," I say. "I'm so glad something good could come out of this."

"Something good definitely has come of it," Monsieur Goldberg says, lifting his cookie and toasting Margot with it. "The single best cookie in all of Paris, I tell you, the best!"

Margot's cheeks are so red and round, they look like balloons. "I'm so happy Levi was found," she says. "Will he be okay?"

"Yeah, he'll be fine once he gets home."

"And you go home today?" she asks.

"Yes."

Now it feels real. Leaving Paris. The real Paris isn't the Paris of my early dreams—the sweeping grandeur of Versailles and the tingly gaze of haughty French boys—but it's infinitely more beautiful than all that. I see that beauty in Margot's smile. I taste it in the croissant she gives me.

And when she says "I have something for you," and brings me a gift bag, I see it again in two beautiful copies of the same book. *The Hunchback of Notre Dame.* One in English, one in French.

"You said you want to read it, so I bought you the French, and I thought to have the English too would help."

I hug her again. I don't want to let go.

When I can finally force my sniffling, teary self to hobble out of the bakery on my crutches, book bag swinging from my hand, I run into Bald Guy on the street. He's angling toward the bakery.

"Are you going in here?" I blurt out. "Seriously?"

He scowls, but nods.

"*Leurs croissants sont bons,*" he grunts as he opens the door and goes inside.

*Their croissants are good.*

"Amen!" I cry.

He looks at me like I'm insane. I think I might be.

⁂

I see Levi for the first time again at Charles de Gaulle airport. Mom brought him, Josh brought me. I had to give the crutches back to the hospital, so I'm feeling embarrassed in an airport-issue wheelchair. Levi is in pajamas and a parka, though, so we're about the same on the ridiculous scale.

"Hey," I say to him as Mom and Josh go to figure out how to check in.

"Hi," he says.

"Do you like my ride?"

"Yeah."

I—carefully, very carefully—twist the wheels so I spin in a circle.

"Lame," Levi says.

"You should get one. We could race."

"They wouldn't give me one. I just need drugs."

I laugh weakly, but it's not funny. At all. Levi tucks his hands into the parka.

"Did they give you that coat at the hospital?"

He snuggles his ears down into the collar of the coat and nods.

"Nice."

Mom and Josh come back, tickets and boarding passes in hand, and there's a lot of hemming and hawing about how to go through security and eventually get onto the plane. I guide us through all the steps. Luggage check. Security. Customs. I tick the boxes on all the forms.

We separate into two lines for customs agents. Josh and Levi in one, me and Mom in the other. "You know your stuff," she says, looking at the throngs of people all around us. "My head spins just looking around this place."

"I guess there are some things I'm capable of handling."

Mom playfully smacks my shoulder. "Shh. None of that."

We clear customs, and Mom immediately scoots behind me to roll my chair.

"I can definitely handle my own wheelchair, Mom," I protest.

"I'm all for helping you realize how capable you are, honey," she says, steering me ahead at a quick clip, "but if I let you push this chair with a sprained wrist, I'm a terrible mother."

❧ ❧ ❧

We take up a whole middle row on the plane. Levi and I sit between Mom and Josh. The flight attendants give us extra pillows and blankets, and we're in one of the rows with extra leg room. All tucked in with no strangers surrounding us—it's miles better than our last flight.

Mom gets out the magazines she bought in the terminal but falls asleep almost immediately. Josh puts on his noise-canceling headphones to listen to the latest epic fantasy bestseller on audiobook. I have my two copies of *Hunchback of Notre Dame* on the little tray table in front of me, but I turn to Levi instead. He's just looking around.

"Hey, Levi."

He looks at me, raised eyebrows his only reply.

"Did I . . . did we have a good time?"

He blinks slowly.

"Well, yeah," he says, incredulous.

"Really?"

"Yeah. It was good."

I'm not going to get much more than that by way of a reply, but I don't really want more.

"It was, wasn't it?" I say softly.

Levi nods and snuggles down further into his blankets, sighing deeply. I open the French copy and start to read.

As the plane jerks to life, beginning its taxi to the runway, Levi's head droops and nestles against my shoulder. I glance at him. He isn't sleeping; he's wide awake. The pressure of his head on my shoulder tells me everything he's never going to be able to say.

I use the words he can't.

"I love you, Levi," I tell him.

He grunts.

THE END

# ACKNOWLEDGMENTS

An acknowledgments section is probably the closest I'll ever come to an Oscar acceptance speech, so please imagine me standing on a stage in a gorgeous dress, clutching a golden statuette and gasping the following words into a microphone.

The first thanks have to go to my agent, Rebecca Podos, for her incredible insight and intuition. Thank you for really *getting* Keira and Levi and helping me bring out the nuances in their relationship that I felt but hadn't been able to bring to life on the page. This is a much better book because of you.

Thank you to my editor, Nicole Frail. In a world where romances are a much easier sell, I'm so grateful to have found an editor who loves my sibling-focused book. Thanks also to assistant editor Kylie Brien for her hard work and everyone else at Sky Pony Press.

Meghan Congdon deserves a million thanks for being on the receiving end of so many crazy rants, secret confessions, and random thoughts I couldn't share with anyone else. Thank you for sitting in Tim Hortons with me for six hours, reading this book aloud. It was transformative for the manuscript, as well as a ton of fun. I'm a firm believer in platonic soulmates, and I'm so happy I found mine. Texas is so lucky.

Thank you to all the teachers I've had over the years who encouraged my writing, especially grade twelve English teacher Paul Demers. I was lucky enough to spend the majority of my school years in French Immersion, and the class trip to Paris in grade ten helped inspire this book. So a special shout-out to all of my French teachers for planting the seed.

Thank you to the crew and management of Squamish McDonald's, for being my second family.

Shout-out to Andrew McMahon, whose music has been the soundtrack of my life—"I see colors when I hear your voice." Thanks also to Kate Miller-Heidke for "Nightflight" and Regina Spektor for "All the Rowboats," songs which directly informed *Maybe in Paris*.

Thank you to my critique partner, Beth Greaves, who understands my writing like no one else, and Jim Dean and Susan Gray Foster, who also read early drafts of *Maybe in Paris*. If I'm forgetting anyone else who helped out in the very beginning, I'm so sorry—imagine your name written here, too.

Thank you to the Absolute Write Water Cooler for being a huge source of information and support from my earliest querying days.

Thank you to each and every member of my 2017 debut group. Your support and enthusiasm have been incredible. It's been so educational and inspirational to have a whole team of writers on your side who are going through the same things at the same time. I tear up when I think about how bright our futures are and how rich the world will be for all of our books. Special shout-outs to Heather Fawcett, Lianne Oelke, and Jennifer Honeybourn, my fellow Vancouver 2017ers, and Tricia Levenseller, who designed me some kick-ass bookmarks.

Thank you to Dad, Mom, my brother, Scott, and my sister, Grace. I promise that this book contains only grossly exaggerated facsimiles of you guys. Love you!

And finally, thanks to Jon Byerley, who makes sure I eat and sleep—or at least strongly recommends I do so—and gently pushes me back into my chair at my writing desk when I'm wandering around the house all distracted. Love you.